MURDER AT THE MUSEUM
A LEMON LISTER MYSTERY

BY BENNA BOS

Paperback ISBN: 978-1-61929-517-9
eBook ISBN: 978-1-61929-518-6
Hardback ISBN: 978-1-61929-519-3

Flashoint Publications First Edition: December 2023

Printed in the United States of America.

www.flashpointpublications.com

For Benna

CHAPTER ONE

She might die like this, strapped to four dogs pulling her through a grove of Eucalyptus trees on some sort of scent-fueled journey into madness. The thought planted itself in Lemon's brain as a gnarly tree root reached up from between the sparse blades of grass to grab the toe of her sneaker and send her flying toward the trunk. As her shoulder smashed into the tree trunk and her face scraped against the pale, peeling bark, she regretted the moment she'd agreed to take over the dog-walking business.

The hands-free dog leash system she used to enable her to walk multiple mutts at once squeezed her torso. The set-up protected the dogs from getting loose, but in this moment, did little for her own wellbeing. Fighting the force of the combined weight and power of 150 pounds of dog, she shimmied herself to an upright position, using the tree as a counterbalance to the incessant tugging.

No amount of whistling or yelling took the slightest bit of attention away from the dogs' hunt. Whatever small, swift animal had caught their focus was keeping it. Lemon wouldn't stand a chance until the thing was safely teasing them from an out of reach tree branch.

The strip of trees wedged between the museum parking lot and the hill leading to the golf course was no wider than a four-lane highway. Nevertheless, the dogs managed to keep their trek in that small rectangle as they dragged her through the length of the grove in pursuit of their prey.

Giving in to the inevitable, she pushed off the tree and pumped her legs, keeping her knees high in an attempt to prevent another face plant. She was at the dogs' mercy now, following their lead. Milo served as battalion commander, his Bassett Hound DNA guiding his every move with his nose. The mini-doodle, pittie mix, and schnauzer all hustled along behind him, just happy to be in on the adventure.

Milo must have found his mark, because the tugging suddenly ceased. Furry bodies gathered in a huddle, blocking Lemon's view of the catalyst for her skinned knees and aching shoulder.

As the fog infused air drifted off the Bay and rolled up the steep embankment to spread like cool, damp fingers through the tree stand, Lemon caught her breath. It felt nice to stand still for a moment after the chaos of the canines' chase.

She chose to ignore the dirt flying at her, covering her shoes and the cuffs of her jeans. It didn't matter right now. She needed a minute. And she was going to take it. But as the dirt pile grew and the dogs' heads dipped further down into the growing hole, she knew she had to stop them. She'd need to find a way to fill in their tripping hazard, and since she wasn't prone to carry a shovel in her backpack of doggie supplies, she was going to be left with a monumental job.

Using a combination of calls, treats, and outright begging, Lemon managed to get all four dogs away from the hole. Milo was the last to give up, his long ears caked with mud, he finally dragged his head away for a piece of dried liver.

Lemon tied the dogs to the biggest, sturdiest tree she could find, certain they might actually be able to pull over a lesser one, and turned her attention to the hole. With each step of her approach, it grew deeper. The crater seemed to recede into the earth. She drew closer, hoping to see the bottom of the pit.

Standing over the chasm, she was impressed with how little time it took four dogs to make such remarkable headway. She might have sighed in defeat at the monstrous task she would have to backfill their makeshift construction site. She might have done or thought a number of things. Instead, as she peered into that hole and saw what lie at the bottom of it, she screamed.

"You found what now?" the 911 operator asked.

Whether it was because of her multi-tasking—the act of texting Mei at that very moment—or because she was holding the phone down and shouting toward it through the breezy afternoon air, or simply because she was completely flooded with panic, Lemon yelled, "A foot! A human foot!"

Having scrambled to untangle the dogs at the frantic pace of the Keystone Cops—her panicked movements far too fast and clumsy— she broke out of the woods to plant herself in the parking lot of a busy museum. And that's when she discovered she had an audience.

A family with two small children, an elderly couple, and a man just pulling himself off his bicycle stood in a clump on the asphalt. They all stared at her, but she really didn't have time to explain her sudden and disheveled appearance.

"Okay, ma'am," the dispatcher said, "what is your name and where, exactly, are you?"

Lemon hit send on her text to Mei and brought the phone closer to her ear. "My name is Lemon Lister."

"Lemon Lister? Really?"

"Yes, really. And I'm in the parking lot of the Legion of Honor, right on the edge, near the golf course."

"You found a foot in the parking lot?"

"No. No. I found it in the trees about…like a little ways from the parking lot."

"Okay, Ms. Lister." The operator's infuriatingly calm voice poked at Lemon's rising frustration. She closed her eyes to attempt to steady herself, but all she could see behind her eyelids was that pale, dead, foot, its delicately painted toenails peering up at her from the bottom of the hole. "And how far away are you physically right now from the item?"

Calling a severed human foot an item didn't really square, but that wasn't the issue at hand. "I suck at distances," Lemon confessed. It was one of several reasons she'd graduated last year with a degree in Communications rather than something that required anything impossible like geometry.

The dispatcher sighed. "Try to guess. Twenty yards? Fifty feet?"

"Literally no idea. I can show someone when they get here."

"I have an officer on the way."

"Just one? For a foot?" Lemon realized as soon as the question left her mouth that she had answered it for herself. Yes. Just one. For a foot. Afterall, you probably needed a whole leg for two cops.

"Ma'am. Are you alone?"

"No, I have four dogs with me."

"Four dogs?"

"Yeah. And my best friend should be here soon."

"You called someone?"

"I texted her."

There was a lot of clicking on the other line. It didn't pause when the operator spoke again. "And how far away is that person?"

Lemon glanced at the courtyard. The massive Rodin statue blocked her view of the front door, but she was certain it would open at any minute and Mei would come flying out. "Not far, she works in the Legion."

"Okay. So please stay where you are. The officer is on his way. Can you give me a description of yourself?"

"I'm five-seven with short, curly brown hair, rainbow sunglasses, a navy windbreaker, and I have the four dogs with me. You can't miss me."

"Very good. Do you want me to stay on the line with you?"

The question probably sounded as silly to the operator as it did to her. But it was a testament to the distress in Lemon's voice. Honestly, though, as much as she liked not feeling alone in that moment, what was going to happen? The foot's owner was going to show up and demand she give it back or else?

"No. I'm good. I'll be right here."

The operator thanked her and hung up. Lemon lowered the phone, still clutching it in her hand. The dogs, long since bored with her drama, had all dropped down around her like a pile of puppy rubble. They lounged on the bumpy, black asphalt as if it were pillowy rubber.

Once the call ended, an eerie silence descended upon on their little gathering. The looky-loos had all made their way into the museum or driven off in their cars. After a beat, a single car door closing punctuated the quiet with its muted thud. But it did little to keep Lemon from feeling utterly alone.

Lemon stared down at Milo. A long ear draped over his eyes like one of those sleep masks her mother always wore on long plane flights. The image of her mother's face—smooth and sun-kissed—pelted her mind, followed by the overwhelming desire to get a motherly hug. But that wouldn't be happening, not today, and not anytime soon.

"Lemon!"

She raised her head. Mei ran through the arched entryway to the courtyard and out into the parking lot with abandon. Her dark hair flew behind her as she rocketed past cars toward Lemon.

The dogs sprang into action. Snickers, the mini-doodle, started the barking. Gemma, the schnauzer, and Tito, pittie-mix, were quick were join in. Milo was slow on the uptake, but a few seconds later his low baying accompanied the others.

Mei came to an abrupt stop a good ten feet from Lemon, providing a comfortable amount of space between her and the barking dogs. She held her arms against her chest and shouted over the noise. "Are you okay?"

"We need to work on your fear of dogs," Lemon shouted back.

"Okay. Not right now. What's going on?"

Since shouting that she discovered a severed human limb was

something Lemon wasn't interested in doing twice in one day, she directed her efforts to settling the dogs. Their instinct to protect her against the terrified five-foot-nothing, ninety-pound sprite before them was just ridiculous at this point.

Mei waited, hands clutched to her chest as if she were protecting them from Cujo himself, while Lemon worked to get each dog to sit quietly. A fistful of treats finally did the trick, and Mei moved a couple steps closer, still staying out of reach of the terminus of the leashes.

"What the hell?"

At least Lemon could hear Mei in the absence of the barking.

"I found a foot! A human foot!"

"Jesus. I thought maybe there was some kind of tragic autocorrect at work on your text. For real? Where?"

Lemon pointed toward the clump of trees that lay innocently between them and the steep hill leading to the golf course, and beyond that, the Bay. Mei glanced in that direction, but of course, she couldn't see anything.

"I'm going to look."

Lemon shrugged. "Be my guest."

Lemon was perfectly happy standing back with her charges and watching the discovery be made by someone else. Sharing the burden, that's what her mother would call it. It reminded her of the time her mother found naked pictures of her grandparents and made her aunt look at them so she wasn't the only one living with that trauma.

Lemon tracked Mei's movements as she hurried to the edge of the sidewalk, stepped off into the grass gingerly, and disappeared in the trees. A moment later a cry echoed back to Lemon just before Mei reappeared.

So disturbed by what she'd seen, Mei ignored her fear of the dogs and sprinted toward Lemon, landing at her side and nestling herself between Milo and Gemma. "What the hell was that?"

Lemon attempted to translate the image in her head into words, but before she could a police car rolled to a stop within spitting range of the two women. This alarming action, however, had no effect on the dogs, who sat in silence even as the car door opened and a man stepped out.

Despite driving a fully marked police cruiser, the man himself wore a simple pair of grey slacks and white button-up shirt with a non-descript grey tie. No uniform. No shiny badge.

He moved casually toward the human and dog gathering, still eliciting zero fucks from the canines. As he approached Mei, he stretched out his hand. She managed to unwind her arm to accept his handshake.

"I'm Detective Zahn. Thank you for calling."

It struck Lemon as odd that he was saying thank you. For what? For calling in a foot? She tried to fathom what other response a person might have to such a discovery. It also occurred to her that either no one had passed along her description to the detective or he merely hadn't paid attention. Small, cute, Mei looked nothing like the robust five-foot seven-inch Lemon.

"I, um, didn't call." Mei's neck craned as she gazed up at the man who towered at least a foot over her. His grey beard and matching head of salt and pepper hair gave him the look of a man who'd seen a lot— probably a lot more than a foot buried beneath a tree. "She did." Mei shoved her thumb toward Lemon.

Detective Zahn took a few steps toward Lemon, fully breaching the dogs' circle of trust. They did nothing. Lemon shook his hand as well. "Hi."

"You're the caller, then? Lemon Lister?"

"Yes, sir."

One side of his mouth quirked up. "Oh, no need to call me that. You can call me Zahn. Can you show me what you found?"

Lemon nodded. She forced herself to move from their safe little spot near the cars to venture back to edge of the parking lot. The dogs followed easily. This time, Lemon used cues and treats to keep them from leaping toward the smell of decaying flesh. She stopped at a spot that put them closest to the horrifying discovery without having to step off the asphalt herself and pointed toward the tree that served as the marker for the offensive pit. "There."

Detective Zahn approached the tree. He returned to the edge of the parking lot a moment later. "Looks like a foot, alright. Probably severed."

Lemon had never considered that the foot might be attached to a body buried even further in the hard soil. Her brain had somehow registered immediately that there was no way a body could've been shoved into that space between the tightly packed trees in the thick soil without significant scarring of the grassy spaces in between.

"So, where's the body?" Mei asked, pulling the words right out of Lemon's mouth.

"Good question." Detective Zahn took a step back, straightened up, and spoke into the radio clipped to his shoulder. After a string of incomprehensible speak that included numbers and letters, he said simply, "Yep. It's a foot. Better send CSI."

Lemon's thoughts were with the dogs. The back of the van was equipped with numerous fluffy dog beds and an air conditioning unit. And the canines were clearly happier snoozing there than hanging out on the pine needle riddled ground near the creepy foot hole. But at some point, she was going to have to get them all home, preferably before their pet parents returned from work.

She imagined the conversations she was going have. "Hey, super sorry, but your dog dug up a human foot in the Presidio today and we had to wait for the cops." She already basically had that discussion with Milo's owner and Mei's boss, Chief Curator of Antiquities, Ron Killian.

Ron came out to see what was up after Mei fled the museum in a hurry and didn't return.

"Is everything all right?" Ron glanced around at the scene.

"Oh, yeah, it turns out that the dogs found something weird is all." Lemon's internal war about whether or not to reveal to Ron that his dog found a human foot resulted in vagueness to the extreme.

"Oh. Okay." Ron patted Milo on the head. "Good luck." He left with a casual wave and headed back into the museum.

So, yeah, that was awkward.

Fifteen minutes later, Lemon and Mei sat on a worn wooden picnic table not far from where a handful of police officers had gathered, a flimsy yellow ribbon wrapped around the trees in a wonky rhombus shape, declaring "CRIME SCENE DO NOT CROSS."

Unaware of the drama, the dogs were happily tucked into the van. Lemon frantically texted her other clients, the ones whose dogs she was supposed to pick up after her walk with the fab four. The last walk of the day consisted of a group of six small dogs. Lemon had nicknamed them the Tiny Terrors because all were teacups or minis who loved to run around the little fenced-in dog park near her apartment. They weren't going to get that chance today, and there would be a handful of clients arriving home to anxious puppers in need of a release.

Lemon was in mid-response to one dog mama when Mei pounded on her upper arm. "Hey, hey, it's Jade."

Lemon glanced up to see the tall, perfectly built blonde strolling through the parking lot toward the crime scene. Dressed in a set of coveralls with a patch indicating her role as CSI for SFPD, Jade Milan looked just as good as she did leading discussions about the latest sapphic novel at their book club gatherings.

Jade didn't appear to notice them. She was about to duck under the yellow tape when Mei shouted, "Jade!"

Lemon's eardrums nearly shattered. Jade spun toward the sound. The large case she carried swung at her side. She raised her free hand and smiled. She left the case, which looked like it weighed eight thousand pounds, on the ground, and strolled toward them. "Hey, what are you two doing here?"

Mei pointed at Lemon. "She found the foot."

"Technically Milo found it."

"One of the dogs you walk?"

A tiny little light of pride burst in Lemon's chest. Jade remembered what she did for a living. She repressed her highly inappropriate grin and nodded.

Jade frowned and shook her head. Soft, blonde curls bounced around her ears. "Sorry you had to see that."

Lemon shrugged. "I mean, you're about to…ya know. Do a lot more than see it."

"Yeah. But I'm used to it. Listen, be safe. I'll see you both soon?"

They waved as she headed back to her job, something both Mei and Lemon needed to do as well. They stared at each other, the unspoken question right there. What the hell do we do now?

"You should go back inside. I'm okay here."

Mei folded her arms over her chest in defiance. "Detective Zahn told us to wait here."

"He told *me* to wait here. That doesn't mean you have to."

"It wasn't clear."

Mei was right about that. Nothing had been clear. They'd been told to stay put, given permission to put the dogs in the van, but received no other instruction. They snuck over to the picnic table on their own, tired of trying to figure out where to stand that was out of the way without being so far away they might be considered fugitives running from the scene of the crime.

Not that it would be possible to slip away entirely. The area had basically become a flashpoint for every visitor to the museum, every biker headed up the path toward the beach, and all the golfers on the attached course. And there they sat, the only civilians allowed inside the carefully maintained police bubble. Inconspicuous they were not.

Lemon's phone dinged. She glanced down to see a message from the owner of Tilly, one of the Tiny Terrors. Nancy was a sweet lady who rarely walked her little dog, so Lemon expected her concern to be for Tilly's missed exercise. Instead, she asked about another dog altogether.

Do you have Snickers?

Snickers the mini-doodle belonged to Nancy's neighbor and best friend, Jillian. Lemon hadn't yet contacted the owners of the dogs that were with her in hopes that she could still return them home without being overly late. But if Nancy knew she was delayed, chances were good Jillian did too. She was probably sitting at Nancy's kitchen table now discussing Lemon and speculating about what could be causing her tardiness.

I do. He's safe and sound.

I was getting worried about him. And Jillian's been gone all day. I'm worried about her too.

Jillian came and went, so it wasn't overly bizarre for her to be gone when Lemon picked up Snickers for his walk. She was a retired executive with a million charity activities. Nancy, on the other hand, rarely left the house. She hired Lemon to take Tilly to the dog park simply so she wouldn't have to do it herself, not because she didn't have time.

Lemon responded to Nancy, *I will text you after I drop Snickers off. I'm sure she'll be home by then.*

"Miss Lister."

Her head shot up. Detective Zahn stood in front of the picnic table. Despite his casual demeanor, his booming voice sounded as though he were about to give a lecture on police procedures to new recruits. "You're free to go." He raised his hand and held out a small, cream-colored business card gripped between two fingers. Please call me if you think of any detail about today you haven't already mentioned."

Lemon took the card from him and tucked it into her pocket. "I will. I promise."

His head bobbed. "Good." Then he walked back to the crime scene.

Lemon and Mei hopped off the table. They picked their way cautiously through the grass, dirt, and strewn tree debris that carpeted the space between the foot hole and the parking lot just as they had seen the investigators do. Without talking about it, Lemon knew Mei was just as disturbed by the thought of potentially treading on a piece of human anatomy as she was.

Lemon stepped onto the black asphalt and all the air that had been trapped in her lungs whooshed out in relief. But then it all went to hell as the breeze carried a conversation from the crime scene to her ears.

The words were as unmistakable as the smooth voice that uttered them. Jade said, "Oh, yeah. I just found the other foot."

CHAPTER TWO

If Snickers weighed more than his twenty pounds, he might have knocked the door down. Anxious to get into his house, and most likely over to his food dish, he scratched frantically at the red paint while Lemon fiddled with the key. She felt bad that he was the last one of the afternoon crew to get dropped off. But it made the most sense because the first dog she picked up for the evening walk of the Tiny Terrors lived right next door. Even though she'd canceled the evening walk after having been dramatically delayed by the police, she kept the dog drop-off and pick-up route the same.

Jillian's beautiful, historic Victorian matched the others in the neighborhood of Sea Cliff. Situated between two strips of Presidio land with a view of the ocean, it was a hell of a place to have real estate. It was also only a few blocks from the Richmond apartment Lemon's parents owned. So when the day after her graduation from college her parents announced they were moving to Belize and handed her the keys to the apartment, Lemon was dumbstruck, but also recognized how lucky she was.

Most twenty-two-year-olds in the city had to live with their parents, like Mei, or work two jobs to share an over-priced 250 square-foot studio with a roommate. Lemon got to live in a paid-for apartment in the Richmond. And as if by magic, her parent's best friend, Madge, decided to follow them to their Central American paradise two weeks later, leaving Lemon the dog-walking business she'd created for her son who'd squandered the gift by landing himself in San Quentin.

So, Lemon had a home and a job to pay the utilities just handed to her. She was grateful, even when her leg muscles ached from the miles of walking or her shoulder hurt from being rammed into a tree by dogs anxious to dig up a human foot.

The wealthy clientele Madge had handed over to her wasn't such a drag either. As Lemon swung open the door to Jillian's house she was greeted by the scent of expensive freshener, not the cheap stuff the rest of the world bought at the grocery store and ripped out of a plastic and cardboard wrapper then shoved into an electrical socket. No, this stuff was high end. And invisible. Despite having looked, more than once, for the source of the aroma, Lemon had yet to locate it in the spacious house.

As soon as Lemon pulled off his harness, Snickers bolted into the kitchen. She slung his gear on the designated hook, because of course Jillian had a special hook—brass no less—for the dog's harness and leash. She moved out of the foyer and into the front room slowly, scanning the space for any sign that Jillian might have come home since Lemon picked up Snickers four hours earlier.

The room was still and quiet, the oil paintings and bay windows glaring back at her as they always did. The stiff couch, covered in a muted red rose pattern, still held the dog blanket in the exact position it had been earlier. The magazine perched precariously on the coffee table still defied gravity.

Lemon called out Jillian's name a few times on her way to the kitchen, with no result. Once she reached the haven of clean tile and stainless steel that was Jillian's favorite room, she spotted Snickers standing in front of his empty bowl, eyeing the ceramic interior, tail pumping, beating against the counter to one side of him.

She'd been doing this gig for three months now, and had learned all the nuances of each client's dog. When Lemon brought Snickers back in the afternoons, Jillian immediately fed him. Lemon stood in the kitchen and watched the ritual several times while talking to Jillian. So, it wasn't difficult to locate his food, measure out the correct amount and give the pup a little relief in the absence of his mom.

During a recent phone call from Belize, Lemon's mother had praised Lemon's uncanny memory for details. She'd related a conversation she and Madge had while lounging on the beach watching her father attempt to surf that involved how Lemon's memory would serve her well as the new owner of Doggo Dilly's. She wasn't wrong.

Of course, there was still the issue of that stupid name. Lemon couldn't afford to repaint the logo on the van right now. So, she was stuck with it for the time being. However, with Dilly himself being incarcerated, it was probably best to take care of that sooner rather than later.

These thoughts drifted through her mind as she toured through the rest of house looking for any sign that Jillian might've come home for at least a quick change of clothes. She never wore the same outfit to two different events. If she'd had an afternoon meeting of one the many committees or boards that she sat on, she would've come home to change before meeting someone for dinner or heading over to a museum or gallery for a special event. More than once, Lemon had arrived to either pick up or drop off Snickers and found Jillian frantically running from her bedroom to her bathroom with heels in her hand and one earring inserted.

There was no such activity now. The house was stiflingly quiet. Lemon was relieved when Snickers finished his dinner and joined her walk through of the house, his nails clicking on the hardwood floor. The family room and both guest rooms were immaculate, as always. The den was perfectly untidy, the antique desk littered with an array of paper and electronics—not overly stuffed, but with enough clutter to indicate an active life.

Lemon felt like an intruder as she followed Snickers through the open bedroom door. He had no such hesitation, immediately jumping up onto the massive king-size bed and plopping down on the pricy comforter. The room was tidy, bed made, dirty clothes tucked safely in the wicker hamper near the door to the ensuite bathroom.

The bathroom door stood wide open. The immaculately clean space was rarely used by Jillian. Lemon knew this because Jillian had once complained while running from the bedroom into the hall bathroom wearing only a slip and a silky blouse that the ensuite was too small to fulfill the needs of her beauty regimen.

Seeing no clues as to where Jillian might be, Lemon swung back out. Snickers decided to stay put, ready for a nap after all the excitement. But that wasn't going to cut it. Until Lemon heard from Jillian, Snickers would need to stay with her. She ducked back into the bedroom and scooped up the pooped puppy.

As she moved back down the hallway, Snickers tucked under her arm, Lemon paused at the main bathroom. The door was cracked open just the tiniest bit. Light spilled out from that slash of space between the door and its frame. Lemon kicked the door with her foot. It swung open and hit the spring stopper on the wall.

Lemon took a half step, peering into the large room. A towel hung over the door of the massive glass-enclosed shower. The vanity was crowded with make-up, hairbrushes, curling irons, and tall, metal bottles filled with a variety of beauty products. Lemon was about to pull her gaze away from the cluttered counter when one tiny object caught her attention.

She spun back around, her eyes pinned to the little glass bottle. A jar of nail polish wouldn't have garnered her attention under any other circumstances. But her memory made a clear and unmistakable connection. The color of the nail polish in that jar was an exact match for the toes of the disembodied foot.

As Lemon entered Nancy's house, just steps away from Jillian's, Tilly attempted to climb up her calf. The dog's high-pitched bark accompanied each bounce from her tiny legs. Snickers nestled further into Lemon's elbow, showing no interest in being put at the mercy of the Yorkie. Lemon's arm was starting to ache, but she obliged the brown, curly mop in her arms as she entered Nancy's sitting room.

Nancy gestured to an overstuffed armchair and Lemon dropped herself and Snickers into it. Fortunately, Nancy stopped the attack from Tilly by scooping her up and tucking her into her lap as she perched opposite Lemon on a patterned loveseat.

"Jillian's not home, is she?" Nancy glanced pointedly at the dog snuggled in Lemon's arms.

"No. Have you heard from her?"

Nancy shook her head, the tight curls of her perm rippling like waves in a jug that was bounced around in the back of a truck. "I've been calling all day. It just goes straight to her voicemail. At first, I figured she was in a meeting. She had two today. But it just kept happening all day. Voicemail every time I called."

Lemon leaned forward. Snickers shifted to accommodate her new position. Tilly prepared to pounce, but all six pounds of her were held at bay by Nancy. "What do you know about her schedule today?"

Nancy's eyes narrowed and her teeth sunk into her lower lip. "It's Thursday, which means she had an afternoon board meeting for the historical society. That should have been it, but then last night she told me she had an early morning meeting. She wanted me to feed Snickers if she wasn't back by the time I took Tilly out for her morning piddle. I went over there, but saw no sign of her."

"Do you know anything about the morning meeting?"

Nancy shrugged, her shoulders nearly touching her ears before falling again. "She didn't say. It could be anything. The museum, the zoo, the homeless shelter, take your pick. That woman is so busy. No idea how to retire."

While Jillian had been a very busy tech CEO before retiring, Nancy had been the empty nest socialite wife of a CEO. To Nancy, retiring meant that her husband died and she didn't have to entertain on his behalf anymore. It was no surprise to Lemon that they had different concepts of how to enjoy their golden years.

"Did she come home to change between meetings?" Even before she asked it, this question had lingered in Lemon's mind. No evidence in the house suggested a midday visit home. It bothered her.

"I never saw her. What about when you picked up Snickers?"

"No. House was locked and dead quiet. I saw that Snickers hadn't had an accident so I figured either Jillian hadn't been gone long or she'd come home. But I guess you let him out."

Nancy's frown spoke volumes. She was worried. So was Lemon. In her arms, Snickers snored.

"Well, that's it then." Nancy stood, taking a squirming Tilly with her. She walked over to an ornate table squeezed between the couch and the wall and picked up her cell phone. "I'm going to make a missing person's report."

"Don't you have to wait, like, twenty-four hours or something?" Lemon asked.

Nancy's nose scrunched up. "I'm not following a stupid rule like that."

"Well, um, should I go back next door and get a picture of Jillian or something?" Images of police officers standing in Nancy's crowded living room asking for a tattered polaroid like they were in a noir detective film flitted through Lemon's mind.

"Okay. But wait until I make the call. I want to be sure I get all the details right."

"Wait. What details? Maybe we should go through them before you call." Comparing notes before they brought in the big guns was a wise move in Lemon's opinion, especially after the taste of the police interview she'd received just an hour before.

Nancy pulled open the drawer on the front of a side table that sat beside the couch and removed a small notebook and pen. She flipped a few pages before scribbling down thoughts she dictated to herself.

"Left the house sometime before eight-thirty for a meeting with an unknown person," Nancy said.

"Does not appear to have returned by one-thirty when I arrived to pick up Snickers," Lemon added, giving the poor dog a long stroke. His soft, supple fur under her calloused hands provided her with comfort even as she gave it.

"Was supposed to have a meeting at two. We don't know if she arrived at that." Nancy touched the pen to her lips, her eyes squinted. "I wonder if we could check on that?"

"Do you know anyone on the historical society board?"

Nancy's eyes got big. "Of course I do. Silly me." She scooped up her cell. She typed out a text, the task taking so long Lemon thought she might perish from the pain of watching it.

Then Nancy stared at the screen for what seemed like several long minutes waiting for a response. Lemon took the opportunity to do a mini-meditation. Long, deep breaths filled her lungs. She took stock of her body. Her posture was bad, the warm body of Snickers pressed against her providing comfort, the rise and fall of his little chest acting as a soothing metronome.

"Jillian wasn't at the two o'clock meeting." Nancy's declaration penetrated Lemon's meditative bubble. The stress and excitement in her voice was almost as alarming as her statement.

"Okay. So, missing persons. What do we need to tell them?"

"They'll want a physical description," Nancy said.

"Well, I know where a photo of her is." Lemon had seen the portrait-style photo of Jillian and Snickers hanging just above the rack holding Snicker's walking gear.

"We need that, yes. But more. We should describe what she was wearing, jewelry, birthmarks. That kind of thing."

"How do you know this?" Lemon couldn't resist voicing her curiosity.

"I watch *a lot* of true crime TV."

"Okay. Well. I don't know what she was wearing, but she always had that one ring on." Hesitant to bring up the toe nail polish, which would lead to the foot situation, which Lemon had not yet revealed to Nancy, she started with something simple.

"I can describe that ring. And then there is the mole on her shoulder." Nancy tapped her right arm. "You only see it when she wears a summery dress. But I know it's there. Oh, and the tattoo."

"Tattoo?" Lemon didn't bother to hide her surprise at the image of the well put together former CEO with ink.

Nancy lifted her right leg, which was covered in dark grey, cotton leggings. She pointed to her ankle. "She got it on her fortieth birthday. It was a bit impulsive. But it's pretty."

The image of the foot flashed through Lemon's mind again. She had only seen the toes and a bit of the top of a foot, the rest still buried in the coastal mud. But how much was down there? How much had Jade and her team uncovered?

"Where exactly is this tattoo?"

Nancy shifted on the couch, pulling her foot up on the cushion beside her. She pushed up her pants and shoved down her fuzzy pink sock and pointed to the ball of bone that made up her own ankle. She traced a "C" shape from the top of the bone to the bottom. "Right ankle. It's a set of flowers that curve around like this."

Based on how low on the ankle Nancy indicated the ink was, it might be visible on a foot that had been relieved of the burden of the rest of its body. Lemon pulled her phone and Detective Zahn's card out of her pocket.

Nancy didn't ask what she was doing. Instead, she just watched and waited as Lemon held the phone to her ear and huffed out quick breaths while the ringing echoed through the line.

"Zahn here."

"Detective Zahn. This is Lemon Lister."

"Ms. Lister. Thanks for calling. Did you think of something?"

"Yeah, one of my clients isn't home, um, Jillian Ross, and her friend and I are worried about her, and um…she has a tattoo."

The detective's calm speech pattern shifted just a tiny bit. "A tattoo?"

"Yeah, apparently, she has a tattoo on her ankle. And I wondered…"

"Which side?"

"Right."

"What is it a tattoo of?"

"I guess flowers."

Nancy called across the room. "Forget-me-nots."

"Yeah, Forget-me-nots," Lemon relayed.

There was an excruciating pause. Then Detective Zahn spoke, his tone firm. "I'm going to need you and this friend to come down to the station."

CHAPTER THREE

Lemon explained for the fourth time since she'd arrived at the police station that she hadn't gone home yet, and as a result the curly puppy was still attached to her via a six-foot leather leash. The two officers crouched on the ground, their faces just inches from the puppy's wet nose, didn't seem to care.

"Ms. Lister, Ms.?" Detective Zahn looked expectantly at Nancy.

"Nancy Millburn."

"Thank you for coming in." Detective Zahn gave the dog only a cursory glance before gesturing for Lemon and Nancy to follow him.

Lemon managed to extract Snickers from the exuberant officers and the tip tap of his little nails accompanied the heavier sounds of three pairs of human feet on the cheap linoleum floor as Detective Zahn led them down a long corridor. Every few steps, under the sickly yellow of the florescent lighting, the recesses cast a shadow on closed doors flanking both sides.

After walking for a what seemed like an eternity, an acrid scent that reminded Lemon of science class penetrated the hall, enveloping them in an inescapable cloud that burned Lemon's nose. Detective Zahn stopped suddenly and turned to his left, gripping a doorknob and shoving open a non-descript entry. "Ladies, I am going to ask you to identify something. Okay?"

Lemon and Nancy both stilled. So did Zahn. Eventually, Nancy pointed her finger at Zahn. "Well, let's get on with it."

Instead of walking in, Zahn stood to the side and held out his arm. Lemon thought the whole scene was a bit too reminiscent of a horror movie for her taste. Nancy didn't share her skepticism. She plunged into the room, leaving Lemon with no choice but to follow.

Sandwiched between the septuagenarian and the police officer, she moved into a harshly lit room stinking of something awful and foreboding. Surprisingly, it held an unexpected pleasure.

Jade Milan stood behind a shiny metal table which held an object draped in a white cloth. Lemon didn't want to think about the hidden horror on that table, so she focused on Jade's high cheekbones and piercing hazel eyes instead.

Jade smiled at her briefly before clearing her throat and straightening her shoulders. Unlike the causal wine-drinking, romantic suspense-loving woman she presented to the book club, this Jade was all business, with a hint of appropriate sympathy.

"Thank you so much for coming. I apologize that we have to do this." Her mouth formed the most perfect frown. "But we need you to see if you can identify a tattoo."

Nancy reached out and grabbed Lemon's hand. Lemon wasn't usually the touchy-feely type. And holding hands with a client was definitely on her "weird" list. But this entire situation had gone far past weird into bizarre territory. So, she squeezed Nancy's hand in what she hoped was a reassuring gesture.

"I'm ready," Nancy said.

Jade said, "Please take a look and let me me know if this is the same tatoo you remember seeing on your friend.

"Okay," Nancy said, giving Lemon's hand another squeeze.

Lemon really wished Jade would get this over with already. The smell in this room was making her queasy. She opened her mouth in an attempt to breathe that way, but the thought of allowing the floating death particles into her mouth was overwhelming and she shut it again.

"I am only going to show the tattoo," Jade said.

Lavender toenail polish rushed through Lemon's head. The same polish she'd seen in Nancy's bathroom. The exact shade she'd seen on the toes of the foot Milo found. She didn't need to see either again. She knew they matched. She didn't mention it though. She decided to bring the nail polish up later, when they were no longer in this nightmare of a room.

Finally, Jade lifted the white cloth and folded it over on itself. All she revealed was a rough, calloused heel, the pale dip that made up the Achilles above it, and the round anklebone creating the hill above the valley. And right there, in that small space, was an elaborate tattoo of a vine wrapped in an arch around the ankle, featuring an array of tiny, blue forget-me-nots.

Nancy swayed on her feet. She squished Lemon's hand. Snickers must have sensed the doom-filled moment because he barked. "That's it! That's her!" No sooner had the words escaped her mouth than her eyes rolled back. Detective Zahn caught her before she hit floor.

The interview room was small and cramped, but a thousand times more comfortable than the dead foot room. Lemon, Nancy, and Snickers all sat together, opposite Detective Zahn. Snickers was over it all and had fallen asleep on Lemon's foot. Nancy was shaking. Lemon sipped lukewarm coffee someone had brought her.

"We will, of course, confirm your identification with DNA. But, in the meantime, we're assuming the victim is, in fact, Jillian Ross."

"Is it possible…" Lemon swallowed hard. "Is it possible she's alive, just, you know, without her feet?"

"The experts say she was dead before the feet were…severed."

Lemon flinched. One more terrible image to add to the collection. "How can we help?"

"Let's start with what you know about her movements today," Detective Zahn said.

Lemon prepared herself to recite everything she and Nancy had run through earlier. She took a deep breath and opened her mouth, but Nancy beat her to it. "I know who killed her."

Lemon and the detective both looked at Nancy. Even Snickers woke up to stare at her.

Detective Zahn said, "Okay. Please tell me,"

"When Jillian was sixteen, she and her boyfriend were parked." Nancy leaned over the table toward the detective. "It was 1968. It was a dark, moonless night. A man approached their car." Nancy paused.

Zahn rolled his finger in a circle. "Go on."

"She saw the shadow of a man over her boyfriend's shoulder. She screamed. The boyfriend turned and the man pointed a gun at them. The boyfriend—I think his name was Howard—he panicked and for some reason opened the car door. The door slammed into the guy with the gun and he was knocked to the ground. Then the boyfriend started the car and got them the hell out of there before the man could get up."

The silence stretched out like taffy until Detective Zahn leaned back in his chair. "That's quite a story. I'm not sure I understand the connection, though."

"Don't you see?" Nancy asked. "It's the Zodiac killer. Jillian just barely escaped being a victim!"

"Hmmm. That is interesting. But what does it have to do with her disappearance today?"

Nancy sighed. Her expression was one of a person having to deal with a three-year-old asking impertinent questions. "Isn't it obvious?"

"Afraid not, ma'am." Detective Zahn's sentiments echoed Lemon's own.

"The Zodiac. He came back to finish the job."

Snickers tugged on the leash, anxious to get back to a soft, warm couch or bed. He didn't seem to care whose it was, as long as he could close his tired eyes. Lemon agreed. It had been a hell of a day.

Her stomach protested that it needed attention first with a low growl that erupted just as she and Snickers rounded the corner and spotted Mei sitting on the steps in front of her building with a big paper bag on her lap. Lemon recognized the bright yellow tag stapled to the top.

"I love you more than you will ever know."

Mei smiled. "Thought you might be hungry."

The three of them, with the aromatic bag in tow, made their way into the narrow entryway that held mailboxes, a steel trashcan, four doors, and a spiral staircase. They loped up the stairs to the second floor where a spacious apartment that still held the stately charm of the 1920's awaited them.

As much as she would have loved the comfort of a parent after a day like this, Lemon was equally grateful that they'd left her the apartment. In a way, walking into it was like walking into a hug from her parents. They'd purchased the cozy unit, in a prime location, back before Lemon was born and before real estate prices in San Francisco required early investment in Apple computers to be affordable.

So instead of coming home to a tiny studio equipped with two pots, a futon, and a dying spider plant, she returned to this amazing home. After ushering them all through the door, she unhooked Snickers. The dog immediately began a thorough examination of the apartment with his keen nose.

Mei dropped the bag on the kitchen island and headed straight for the cupboards. Lemon plopped into one of the retro vinyl barstools and slumped onto the counter. "What a fucking day."

Mei pulled out a couple plates and set them gently on the island beside the bag. "How was the police station?"

"Charming. I got to see the foot again, this time a whole new view. So yay. And then Nancy solved the case."

Mei looked up from the utensil drawer. "She did?"

"Yeah. Can you grab a bowl and fill it with water for Snickers?"

Mei did as Lemon requested. "So Nancy solved the case?"

"Oh, yeah. Totally solved it. The Zodiac Killer did it."

Mei laughed. "Oh, really?"

"Yep. Really. So, I'm sure the cops are pleased."

Mei shuffled through the unorganized half of the silverware drawer. "I bet. Did she happen to know who the Zodiac is?"

"Yep. Arthur Leigh Allen, of course. She saw it in a movie."

"Okay. Isn't he dead?"

"Nancy admitted that was a flaw in her theory."

Mei laughed again. "Wow. That was productive."

Lemon's melancholy seeped back in. "It was in one way. They say Jillian is definitely dead."

Mei finally located two matching pairs of chopsticks. She held them up in triumph for a brief moment before her face fell. "Sorry. That sucks. I don't suppose they found the rest of her?"

"No. 'Fraid not." They both turned to watch Snickers paw at a throw pillow on the couch. The poor baby had no idea he was an orphan now.

"You're keeping him, right?"

"Of course. Unless Jillian's son wants him, I guess."

"Shit. I forgot she has a kid. And an ex-husband, yeah?"

"Ex-husband ran off to Sweden with his secretary like fifteen years ago. I doubt anyone'll hear from him." The memory of Jillian cursing her ex while cutting an onion flooded Lemon's brain.

Mei set one pair of chopsticks in front of Lemon and shoved another set to her right. Then she took a pair of scissors out of Lemon's junk drawer and cut open the paper bag. It occurred to Lemon that this was one of the great advantages to having a best friend. They knew where everything was in your house.

Mei asked, "What do we know about the son?"

Awesome thing about having a best friend number two: everything is "we."

"His name is Mike. He's an engineer in his early forties, but his wife is like our age, maybe a little older. Her name is Tina, and Jillian told me she hates her. That's all I know."

"Well, I mean, who doesn't want to kill their mother-in-law and cut her feet off then bury them outside an art museum." Mei shrugged before sliding a plate burdened with Orange Chicken, Kung Pao, and a massive egg roll over to Lemon.

Politeness took a backseat to hunger as Lemon brandished her chopsticks and dug into the Orange Chicken first. Mei filled her own plate and swung around the island to sit beside Lemon.

They ate in silence. Snickers gave up his Lewis and Clark-like journey of the house to sit between their feet in hopes of scoring a dropped morsel.

"I know Jillian was the president of the museum board, but that's about it." Mei brandished her chopsticks toward Lemon. "I've seen her at the museum a couple times, but I've never actually even met her. What do you know about her?"

Lemon swirled rice noodles around her chopsticks. "I liked her."

"You like everybody," Mei said.

"She was that kind of fierce, badass woman that a lot of people didn't like because she was too intense, you know?"

"The kind insecure men can't handle so they don't vote for?"

"Yeah. That kind. I admired her."

"I've heard the same thing at the museum. Some people hated her and others loved her. No one seems to be real middle ground about her."

Lemon peeked down at Snickers. His head was tucked between his paws. His eyes were closed, and he snoozed quietly, blissfully unaware of all that had changed in one short day.

"Okay, tell me more about her," Mei said.

"She ran her family's company for a long time. And she retired not long ago. I'm not sure exactly when, but not too long before Madge left me the business. She has the one son, but I don't know much about him. I've talked to him on the phone a couple times and once I was at the house picking up Snickers when he came by. He seems nice, like regular, you know."

"Did you meet the daughter-in-law?"

"No. Just heard about her from Jillian. None of it good."

"So, since she was retired, what did she do with her time? I mean, she paid you to walk her dog, so was she busy?"

"Very. She spent a ton of time on charity stuff. She was always running off to meetings and fundraisers. She told me that she used to take Snickers with her everywhere she went, but then one day Snickers bit someone." Lemon carelessly released this information to Mei then immediately regretted it.

Mei raised her feet off the ground as if a mouse had just scampered by. "Are you telling me this thing bites?" She pointed to Snickers, who raised his head lazily. One side of his fuzzy cheek was matted down from slumber, making him look like a mussed up muppet.

"Once. And I don't know who it was but Jillian said they deserved it."

Mei slowly lowered her feet but continued to glare at the little dog.

"Anyway, it happened at the museum, and Jillian realized she needed to leave poor Snickers at home."

Mei raised her feet again. "My museum?"

Lemon sighed. "Mei, he's harmless. Look at him." She pointed to the sleeping twenty-five pounds of curly fluff.

"Says you. But not the person he bit."

"I believe Jillian. I have no doubt they deserved it." She gazed lovingly at the sleeping pooch.

Mei dabbed her lips with a paper towel and completely changed the subject. "So, it was interesting seeing Jade, huh?"

Lemon shoved her plate forward and rested on her elbow. "Not really. I mean, it's her job is to go to crime scenes. And that was definitely a crime scene."

"Oh, so you expected her to show up, did you?"

Lemon shrugged.

"So, you didn't enjoy seeing her?"

Lemon stared at Mei, her eyes narrowed in suspicion. "What are you looking for here?"

"I want you to admit that you have a crush on her. Because it was clear as day on your face today, just as it was the last three times we went to book club."

"So now is the time you choose to force a confession out of me?"

"Why not? Sometimes intense situations clarify emotions."

"Fine. She's hot. So what?"

"Just happy to get the confession is all."

CHAPTER FOUR

Lemon liked to call the six dogs she took out in the morning the "Coffee Crew." In order to gather them all and get to the park by nine, as promised to her clients, she had to leave her apartment at eight. Hence the thermos full of coffee she carried in her backpack along with dog treats, water, and poop bags.

Of the three sets of dogs she walked, this group was the largest. Why six dogs had been scheduled for the morning was a mystery. She fully blamed Madge for making her life difficult.

She'd barely made it behind the closed fence of the dog park and dropped her doggie supplies backpack onto the bench beside her when her phone rang. The ringtone reserved for her parents penetrated the cotton bag. But with six dogs strapped to her waist she had no choice but to let it ring out.

Once all the dogs were freed from their leashes to romp around the enclosed space and make new friends, Lemon planted herself on the hard wooden slats. She needed to call her parents back, but things had to come in order. And the first order of the day was pouring herself a steaming cup of hot coffee.

Once she'd taken enough sips to begin feeling human again, she fished her phone out of the pack and returned the call to Belize.

"Pumpkin!" Her mother's voice floated over the line. And even though she was still suffering from a touch of spite after her parents moved to another continent immediately following college graduation last year when she was still trying to figure out what the hell she was going to do with her life, a streak of affection and warmth ran up her spine.

"Hi Mom. How's it going?"

"We're good. We bought a goat!"

"Oh, wow. That sounds…amazing."

Her father, an environmental lawyer and her mother, a socially responsible investment banker, had done well for themselves while still living their hippy philosophy every day—of course they retired early and took off to Belize to buy goats. What did Lemon expect? Maybe supportive parents like Mei's, who still have dinner with her and talked over her day.

"So, something happened yesterday."

"You mean the foot?"

Lemon was floored. She ripped her gaze away from a tumble of dogs rolling over each other in the center of the lawn to stare at the phone, mouth agape. "You know about that?"

"Jessica called me."

Lemon nearly hit her forehead with the palm of her hand. Her mother's friendship with Mei's mom had clearly spanned across continents. She should have known. "What did she say?"

"That you found a foot."

The words hung there in midair as if they dangled from a string. Mimi the French Bulldog waddled over and poked Lemon with her nose. Lemon reached down and gave her a scratch behind the ears. "So, she told you that, huh?"

"Yeah. Tell me more."

Lemon could practically hear her mother rubbing her hands together in anxious delight as she waited for the gory details.

"Milo found a foot. The police came, and then me and Nancy went down to the station and identified it."

"Nancy? Nancy who?"

"Jillian Ross's best friend. She lives next door."

"Wait. Lemon. What does this have to do with Jillian Ross?"

Lemon was pretty sure that when Detective Zahn told her that the identity of the victim was to remain a secret until they had time to contact the family probably applied to her too, but she didn't know if immediate family counted. Besides the cat was already out of the bag.

"It turns out the foot belongs to Jillian, and the police don't think she's walking around without feet. So, yeah. But it's not public knowledge yet, so don't say anything to anyone in SF, okay?"

"Oh, honey. We're so far away." Says the woman who learned within eighteen hours that Lemon had found a severed human foot.

"Anyway, yeah. It looks like Jillian is…missing."

"I knew Jillian. She was a good patron. A good philanthropist. Not everyone liked her, but she had the City's best interests in her heart and that means something."

"I didn't realize you knew her, Mom."

"Oh, sure. We ran in the same circles, sort of. Anyway, I knew her. What do you think happened to her?"

"I have no idea."

"Listen, Lemon. I knew enough about Jillian to know that you need to look into her son Mike and his much younger wife. I'm telling you, they had everything to gain by her death."

Jasper the uber-mutt started humping a Husky that was not part of Lemon's pack. She called him back, holding her hand over the phone so as not impair her mother's hearing with her loud yell.

"Lemon, did you hear me? You have to look into Mike Ross."

"Mom, I'm not a cop. I'm just a dog walker."

"Look, sweetheart. The SFPD have a lot on their plate. They need help. Who better than you?"

Lemon could think of about a million other people.

Mei once commented that George Nichols looked like a model for sixty-five plus bodybuilding. And Lemon had to admit that his physique had not gone unnoticed, especially since he usually wore short-sleeved shirts at home. But the fact that Mei was able to discern that he kept up a four-times weekly workout routine through the semi-casual clothing he wore to the museum when he was there in capacity as a board member was impressive.

George stood in his foyer and held out his arms. Klee ran directly into them. Towering over both Lemon and Klee, the big man reached down and scooped up the pup. His muscular arms kept Klee safe as he pressed his nose into the thick orange fur at the dog's neck.

"He was good boy," Lemon said. "Did a lot of running this morning."

George gently lowered Klee to the ground. "Any chance you could add him to the afternoon crew today? I need to go down to the Legion of Honor for an emergency board meeting."

"Yeah, how're things going on the museum board?"

"It's a bit of a mess now. Jillian Ross was the board president. Did you hear about what happened to her?"

Unable to juggle what she was allowed to say with what she couldn't and unwilling to end up having to explain any accidental disclosures while sitting on a hard, metal chair in a police interrogation room, she remained vague. "Oh, not really. What happened?"

"You need to check the news. Big deal. She's missing. The police announced it today." George squinted. "Hey, don't you walk her dog?"

Lemon took a step backward toward George's front door. She'd verbally painted herself into a corner she was now attempting to physically walk herself out of. "Oh wow. I need to take a look at the news and make some calls."

"Yeah. Definitely check on that dog, yeah?"

"I will. And I can drop by and get Klee this afternoon as well." She made it to the door and placed her hand on the knob.

"Okay. I probably won't be here. Just use the key."

"You bet." She swung the door open. "Have a good meeting."

Lemon tucked herself into the driver's seat of the van before pulling out her phone. She pressed the news app first. After searching for Jillian by name, she read through three articles, all with the same vague information about a search for Jillian Ross because "something suspicious" had turned up outside the Legion of Honor. They talked about Jillian, her service on the Legion's board, her battle over some internal issues. But there was no mention of Lemon.

Abandoning the news, she did a quick Google search of herself, finding only articles on dog walking and a mention of her college graduation. She heaved a sigh of relief and typed out a text to Mei.

It hit the news.

Mei responded almost immediately. *I know. I saw. Surprised you did.*

Lemon ignored the jab. *My client, George, is also on the museum board.*

You walk George Nichols dog? You didn't tell me that.

I didn't realize it mattered.

OMG. Listen. You have to have a special pass to get into the museum tomorrow. Closed to the public. And all the staff gets one plus an additional. I got you a pass. We totally need to be there for the search.

Lemon typed back, *Search?*

Ugh. Calling.

Mei's frustration with text messaging wasn't new. She frequently stopped mid-conversation and called. It took only a few seconds for Lemon's phone to ring.

"Hey. What's this now?"

"Did you read the news?"

"Yeah. I did." Had she missed something?

"SF Gate?"

Mei's obsession with getting her news from that particular local source was not shared by Lemon. "Uh. No. Whatever was on the app."

Mei sighed. "How many times do I have to tell you that being discerning about where you get your news determines how informed you truly are?"

"Okay. Save the lecture. What does SF Gate say?"

"They're conducting a massive search of the area around the museum and the golf course. Both are closed to the public tomorrow. But our CEO convinced the police to let the staff come in because we have exhibit changes happening. Anyway, passes. The second passes are really meant for vendors or whatever. I plan to spend the day watching the search. Are you in or not?"

Lemon knew Mei didn't usually work Saturdays. As curatorial staff she got the most done on the days the museum was closed. But Saturdays were a busy day for visitors and it was a day most staff had to work. On this Saturday, when they were forced to give out special passes for everyone coming and going due to the crime scene outside, Mei said it was easier for HR to issue passes to all the staff than sort it out, allowing Lemon the chance to sneak on through.

Thirty minutes after she arrived, Lemon, Mei, and handful of other back office staff stood in a clump in the side parking lot watching the massive search. At least three dozen people were standing in a tight group talking over logistics.

With no visitors to attend to, most museum staff spent the time catching up on paper work or cleaning tasks, with easy access to a break to peek in on the drama happening outside.

It was hard to tell who all was involved in the search effort and who was just a looky-loo. So many different uniforms covered the searchers bodies, some displaying bright yellow traffic bibs, others so overladen with equipment their patches and wording were wholly obscured.

Matt, one of the accounting staff at the museum, pointed to one set of searchers. "You know there are a bunch of volunteers in that group. The ones in the green bibs. That's volunteer Search and Rescue. My girlfriend is on the squad, only she's not here today. A lot of them aren't."

"Why not?" Mei asked.

Matt turned to gaze at Mei and Lemon, his bangs swinging like a set of blinds in a heavy wind. "There's like this major training for first responders in San Deigo. And a lot of the SAR volunteers are first responders in their day jobs, like my girlfriend. She's an EMT. So the team is short. This is half of what usually shows up to a major search like this." He waved his hand at the volunteers forming a circle around one man near the picnic table Mei and Lemon had waited at on Thursday.

The group fell silent again as they attempted to hear whatever instruction the man in the center was providing. But his voice did not carry over the space between them. The light breeze off the Bay and the sounds of the city penetrating through the grove of trees created a veil of noise just loud enough to muffle the conversation.

The gaggle of volunteers broke up and split into distinct groups that then walked off together, while the man in the center moved with purpose toward the unwanted audience gathered at the side of the building.

"Oh, shit," Mei said. "I think our fun is about to be over."

Like Mei, Lemon assumed the man was going to ask them to leave the area. But as he approached, he smiled. He stuck his hands on his hips and addressed the dozen people standing there. "We could use some more volunteers. I don't suppose any of you are up to the challenge."

Having already done as much dead body part finding as she would like, Lemon took a step back and shook her head. But Mei tugged her arm, yanking her forward. "We would."

Jack—that was the name of the head SAR guy—had given them a quick and dirty orientation. He admitted that it was a poor substitute for the intensive training his other volunteers had been through, but as long as they followed the directions of their leaders to a "T", it would do for today.

Lemon and Mei were assigned to work with a helicopter pilot named Allison. Her strong frame easily carried a massive backpack stuffed with all manner of equipment Lemon couldn't even begin to name let alone use. Her hair hung in greasy loops around a dusty bandanna wrapped precariously across her forehead.

Fortunately, all Lemon and Mei needed to be responsible for was the operation of a small radio clipped to their belts and their ability to hang onto a rope tethered to Allison.

For a grueling three hours, they crawled slowly over a patch of rough grass at the edge of the golf course. Lemon was responsible for three feet on each side and in front of her. Mei had her own area of land just to Lemon's right, with Allison on the other side of Mei.

More than once, Lemon paused to rub her aching eyes, and several times Mei commented that the people assigned to search the soft, well-cared-for cushion of turf on the golf course should switch places with them.

By the time they stopped to break for water and Kind bars passed out by one of the other volunteers, the knees of Mei's jeans were bright green and Lemon's hands were more raw than they were after a day of wrangling dog leashes.

"So." Mei turned to Allison. "You've done this a lot?"

Lemon couldn't help but notice that as Mei sat down beside Allison on the tree stump they were using as a makeshift bench, her eyelashes batted wildly.

Allison shrugged. "A bit. If I'm off duty, then I put myself on call for SAR. There's something really satisfying about being part of a search. Of course, it's better when you find live people."

"I bet," Lemon said, wishing she'd found a live person instead of a freaking foot.

"But I've found some interesting things."

Mei bounced on her seat. "Like what?"

Allison's eyes grew wide. "One time I found a single bloody sock. Turned out it was evidence in the trial. Another time, we were searching Ocean Beach, and I found the murder weapon, which was a knife, buried under the sand. That was big."

"Oh my God. Did they catch the killer?"

"Unfortunately, no. That was one of those times where you get all worked up for a victory and then it all just falls apart. It was a major bummer."

Mei shoved her thumb at Lemon. "Lemon found the foot, you know?"

Allison leaned over to get a better view around Mei. "You did?"

Lemon was pretty over telling the story, so she just nodded. Mei could tell it. After all, she was the one who clearly wanted to impress Allison. But before Mei could get into narration mode, their radios all squawked, creating a jumbled cacophony. Allison acted quickly. She reached over and flicked off both Lemon's and Mei's radios before turning up the volume on her own.

Jack's voice echoed through the speaker. "We have a find in section six Everyone gather back at the hub so we can re-assign."

"What does that mean?" Mei asked.

"It means they found something, and we're going to concentrate on that area as it's most likely to yield additional evidence."

"So, the thing they found isn't…" Lemon debated how to frame her question. But Allison cocked her head in curiosity, waiting, and Lemon gave up. "The rest of her?"

"No," Allison said. "If that were the case, they'd stop the whole thing and CSI would take over."

"Oh right. That makes sense," Lemon rose from their place of respite and followed Allison and Mei across the area they'd just meticulously searched, up a steep hill, and into a crowd of searchers gathered in a tight ball around Jack.

Being at the back of the circle of bodies might have impeded Lemon's view of Jack and whatever he was doing in the center of the crowd, but it provided her a direct line of sight to the clump of police officers standing on the other side of the picnic tables.

A tall man in a blue uniform pulled away from the group. It wasn't until he was halfway across the empty space between the officers and the gathered volunteers that Lemon realized it was Detective Zahn. He looked younger and grumpier wearing that stiff uniform, but his stride was long and sure.

Certain the detective must be headed for Jack, Lemon nearly catapulted over the edge of the hill they perched on when he locked eyes with her and shifted direction.

Lemon tugged on Mei's sleeve. Zahn stopped near the closest table and waved to her with fingers moving toward his palm. She practically dragged Mei along as she approached the detective. Zahn's face crumpled in an attempt to morph his grouchy frown into a smile. It did nothing to reel Lemon in. But she moved one step at a time toward him, clutching Mei's arm in a death grip.

"What the hell?" Mei asked as they landed in front of the detective.

"Hello Ms. Lister, Ms. Lu. It's nice to see you both again," Zahn said.

Lemon attempted to return the smile, hoping it appeared to be at least slightly more genuine that Zahn's. "Hi, Detective."

Mei nodded casually. "What's up?"

Zahn returned Mei's petulant acknowledgement with a mirrored nod before turning back to Lemon. "I was hoping you'd take a look at something for me."

Lemon's stomach dropped. Her feet vibrated with the desire to run away. She did not want to stare at another body part and try not to imagine it attached to the rest of Jillian. "Um. Okay. I guess."

"Great." Zahn spun on his heal and stomped toward the clump of police.

Unable to run away but not wanting to follow Zahn either, Lemon's feet stuck to the dry grass until Mei turned the tables on her and yanked on *her* elbow. Nearly as soon as they reached the officers, they were encircled in a mass of uniforms.

Finding herself the center of attention pushed Lemon off-kilter. Terrified of doing something embarrassing like fainting in front of all these seasoned officers who'd no doubt seen far worse than a pale, dead foot, she straightened her spine and took in a deep breath.

"Ms. Lister." A young officer stepped forward, a plastic bag in her hands. She presented the bag to Lemon. "Have you seen these before?"

Lemon's vision swam for a brief moment until she forced it into focus. The plastic bag seemed clearer than any she'd ever seen. Perhaps the police had some special plastic bag supplier with superior technology. Whatever the case, Lemon could see the two muddy shoes inside as well as she could see her own. Only instead of a worn-in pair of Chucks, the high heels were practically new.

Despite the splotches of mud clinging to the thin heels and the pointed toe, it was obvious that the gray fabric had been little used prior to its encounter with the elements. The color and shape of the shoes seeped into Lemon's memory.

In her mind she could see the shoes as they hung by their heel straps from long fingers. The sharply pointed toes dangled beside the hem of a pencil skirt. All the while Jillian explained that Snickers was suffering from a bout of diarrhea.

Lemon sucked in as much air as she could get in that tight circle and said, "Yes. I recognize them."

CHAPTER FIVE

Lemon had never looked forward to Book Club so much in her life. Three sleepless nights and a few deeply disturbing days were about to be rewarded with a night with the girls talking about the latest and greatest in Sapphic books.

The only problem was that she hadn't actually read this month's assigned book. She revealed this within a few minutes of meeting up with Mei at the 16th Mission BART station.

"I think you will be forgiven," Mei said as they rose out of the dim station and into the twilight. "You've had a shitty week."

"I did start the book," Lemon said. "Got to chapter four."

Mei chuckled. "Sorry, honey. This is one of those books where everything happens in the last half." Mei side-stepped a broken needle on the sidewalk and skipped up to the crosswalk. "Pretty cool that this month's club is being hosted by Jade, huh?" She waggled her eyebrows.

Lemon kept her eyes pinned to the red light warning her not to cross. "I guess."

"Oh, my God! Quit being evasive." Mei elbowed her in the side, nearly sending Lemon into the busy intersection.

Lemon frowned at her friend. "What the hell?"

"You're going to get to see your crush's house. Please don't lie and tell me you aren't curious. I am, and I don't have a crush on her."

The light changed and Lemon moved into the crosswalk. "You have a crush on Lisa. And we've been to her house at least twice since we joined."

"And it was *awesome*. You learn so much about a person when you see the art on their walls."

Lemon shrugged. The art on Jade's walls wasn't at the top of her mind. Despite her need to get away from the drama of the last few days, she couldn't help but want to pick Jade's brain about her missing/presumed dead client. The questions had piled up like a Jenga tower and Lemon couldn't help but hope that pulling the right block might bring her the answers she felt desperate to uncover.

"You know, she probably can't say anything about the case." Mei's casual tone matched her stride as they rounded a corner to put them on Jade's street.

"What? I didn't say shit about the case." Lemon's defensiveness reared up automatically.

"I know. I'm just saying. If you wanted to ask her about it—and I know *I* do—she's probably going to plead the fifth."

"The fifth is for people who don't want to incriminate themselves, not people working on a case," Lemon said.

"Whatever. Instead of losing her right to life and liberty she's afraid of losing her job. Totally understandable. Hey, that's it." Mei shoved her finger toward a cute brownstone.

They took a sharp left turn and walked up the three steps to the red door. Mei operated the buzzer box and secured their entrance. A set of narrow, steep steps later they stood in front of Jade, her front door swung wide open.

It wasn't until Jade captured Lemon in an embrace that she truly comprehended what was happening. The feeling of those strong arms wrapped around her nearly undid Lemon. But it was the words that followed that really made her melt.

"I'm sorry for all you've been through," Jade whispered, her voice soft and smooth in Lemon's ear.

Lemon shivered and nearly died on the spot.

The conversation about the book soothed Lemon. She leaned back in the wine-colored couch, her shoulder pressed against Mei's, and listened to the ebb and flow of voices. She didn't have much to say, having read little of the book herself, but she preferred it that way, it allowed her to drink more wine.

By the time the book conversation wound down, Lemon had lost count of how many glasses of the local pinot noir she'd consumed. But she'd sat through a few cork removals and partook from each bottle. The edges of the room blurred and the words of her fellow book club members reached her ears like floating waves, slow and calming.

She was still in this very chill state, albeit with a glass of water clutched in her right hand, when the book club president approached her spot on the couch. "Hey, Lemon." Hayley said. "Can we talk?"

Lemon swung her head slowly, careful not to send the room into an uncontrollable spin. She'd apparently been lost in a haze when most of the book club members left. Now only her, Mei, Haley, and Jade remained in Jade's cozy apartment.

"Um, yeah, sure."

Hayley sunk into the chair opposite Lemon. The chair to her right was already occupied by Jade, a space Lemon's gaze had wandered to again and again all evening. Alcohol did nothing to inhibit her desire to watch Jade's beauty shine in the room.

Hayley cringed as she spoke. "I heard about your…discovery,"

Lemon's gaze shifted to Jade, who shook her head. "Not from me."

A lock of brunette hair fell in front of one of Hayley's eyes as her head bobbed. "No. Not from Jade. She won't tell me shit."

"Sorry. I value my job."

Hayley glanced at Jade quickly before looking away. "It was from a different source."

In no condition to participate in a guessing game, Lemon let that comment flow past her. "Yeah. Um. I found the foot."

Mei leaned forward. "She sure did."

Excitement grew in Hayley's voice. "And it was Jillian Ross's? That's what I heard on the news."

"That's what they say," Mei said.

Hayley rested her elbows on her knees. "I worked for Jillian, you know?"

Lemon's fog began to clear as a spark of surprise and something even more visceral penetrated her brain. "Wait. What?"

Hayley pulled a glass off the coffee table between them and took a long sip of dark red wine. "Yeah. I was her CPA."

A distant memory hit Lemon. When she and Mei had first joined the club and met Hayley, Mei commented that a lesfic book club run by an accountant had to be good because everyone knew that accountants were calm by day and wild by night.

"I was her dogwalker," Lemon said, her words running together just a little bit.

"I know," Hayley's words were not unkind, just matter-of-fact. "I transferred the money to pay you, at least until last month. That's when I quit."

"Why did you quit?" Mei asked.

Hayley leaned back in her chair. Her mouth turned down. She squinted her eyes. "Let's just say that Jillian and I had a difference of opinion on some things."

A deep silence blanketed the room.

"What the hell does that mean?" Mei asked.

"I'm not at liberty to say anything more than that." After a moment where her gigantic info tease hung there in the air of Jade's living room, Hayley must have realized she'd completely shut down the conversation, putting them all in a corner of awkwardness. She rose. "But, um, I do need to go. I just wondered…" She cleared her throat, stuck a smile on her face, and moved toward the door. "Let me know if you hear anything. I'll be real curious to see how this all turns out. Goodnight."

And then she was gone.

Mei waited approximately one second after the door shut behind Hayley to turn toward Lemon and Jade. "What the hell was that?"

Jade's gaze lingered on the front door. "Strange. That's what that was."

"Awkward AF," Lemon agreed.

Mei clapped her hands. "We *need* to talk about how we just found out that Hayley is connected to the foot lady. I mean, I am dying to know—sorry for the pun—and Lemon is freaking traumatized."

"Jillian," Lemon corrected. "Not the foot lady. Please use her name." She ran her palm over her forehead and fought at the wave of nausea that accompanied the word "foot" these days. Jillian meant more to her than the piece of her she'd found, even if Lemon was just the person who walked her dog. The brief moments they'd shared during pick-ups and drop-offs had given Lemon a glimpse at a woman she admired. And now she was the guardian of the dog Jillian deeply loved. That was a connection Mei might never understand.

Mei reached over and rubbed Lemon's back for half a second. "Sorry. I didn't mean to be insensitive. I'm just a little excited. I mean, don't you all think it's a little crazy that we just found out that Hayley used to work for her? And that she just quit? Right before Jillian ended up dead."

"Mei, Hayley didn't kill Jillian," Lemon's gaze swung to Jade, who sat across from them with a look of deep concentration. "I mean that's just crazy. Right, Jade?"

Jade nodded absentmindedly. "There are few potential suspects."

Mei rubbed her hands together and scooted to the edge of the couch. "Oh, yeah. Like who?"

Jade snapped out of her trance and glanced at Mei. "Honestly, I don't know. I process the evidence, that's it. I don't know anything about the investigation. Though everyone seems to think I do." She shrugged. "My internal detective is just as curious as yours."

"Okay, let's go through all the people we know had a connection to Jillian," Mei said. She held out a finger. "We've got Hayley, Jillian's accountant."

"*Former* accountant," Jade pointed out.

"Right," Mei said. "And there's George Nichols."

Jade's forehead wrinkled adorably. "George Nichols?"

"He's on the Legion's board with Jillian, and Lemon walks his dog."

"Wait," Lemon protested. "Why just George? Why not everyone on the board with her?"

"Because it is a well-known fact around the Legion that George and Jillian are arch-enemies. They've been butting heads for the last few months. Apparently it was over the authentication of a piece."

"Why didn't you mention this before?" Lemon's sense of betrayal echoed in her question.

"I literally just found today when I doing some subtle asking around at work."

Lemon doubted there was anything subtle about Mei's questioning at work. "I mean, that's interesting, but is there anyone else on the board that didn't like her or was upset over this authentication?" Lemon couldn't stomach the thought of George as anything more sinister than a man who didn't like kids messing up his rose bushes by cutting through his yard.

Mei leaned forward. "Not that I know of. Though, I'm pretty low on the totem pole. I'm probably not getting the best info. But even I heard about the George thing. That's gotta mean something."

"But have you met George? Seriously, he's the nicest guy," Lemon said.

Jade raised her finger at Lemon. "Great, he's yours then."

"What?" Lemon's brows rose to her hair line.

Jade pointed to herself. "I'll talk to Hayley. I've known her for years. See what I can get out of her. And you talk to George."

"Talk to him how?" Whatever kind feelings Lemon had toward Jade were fading fast in the face of being tossed into a murder investigation and acting as a spy. Lemon was notoriously nonconfrontational when it came to peer pressure. It's why she got suspended right along with Mei senior year of high school, how she ended up at that stupid party that resulted in the worst haircut of her life, and exactly why she'd go talk to George Nichols about the murder even though it was the last thing on earth she wanted to do.

"Just gently probe him," Jade offered.

Lemon didn't find that the least bit helpful.

Mei jumped in. "Everyone is talking about Jillian right now. And *he* told *you* about the news article. It wouldn't be weird to, ya know, start a conversation with him and see what he says."

Lemon swallowed hard, feeling the pressure of Mei and Jade's expectations. There was only one way out of this trap now—diversion. "What about you, Mei? Who are you going to investigate?"

Mei didn't hesitate. "I'm going to talk to Tina Ross."

"Wait. Ross. Is that Jillian's daughter?" Jade asked.

"Daughter-in-law," Mei said. "And she's a client of my aunt's. Gets her nails done like clockwork every two weeks. I've talked to her before when I was at the shop. I'll arrange it so I'm there next time and try to get her to talk."

Jade grinned. "Sounds like a plan."

Lemon raised her hand in the air. "Can I point out that it's a mildly deranged plan?"

"You certainly can," Mei said. "But it's not going to stop us."

Lemon stared at the swirling dark patterns in the wood grain of the door. Snickers, Togo, and Buttons were counting on her to return to the van soon with Klee, grab Jasper and Jerome and head to the park. Instead, she was standing in front of George's front door paralyzed by indecision.

Rather than delay her day any further, Lemon shoved her task out of her mind, choosing to go with the last minute action plan. Her knock triggered barking from Klee, and it wasn't long before George pulled open the door and invited her in.

"Hey, ready for the morning crew, huh? Well, Klee is all in." George smiled as stepped aside so she could walk through the threshold.

Lemon gave Klee a scratch under his wiry chin and found the exact opening she needed. "I call them the coffee crew, since I drink my coffee while they are playing at the park. Which reminds me, I forgot my coffee."

It was technically true. Lemon forgot her coffee in the van, choosing not to bring it into George's place with her, though she implied that she'd done the unthinkable and actually walked out of her house without a steaming thermos of life-sustaining serum.

"No problem. I got you covered." George turned on his heel and headed to his kitchen. He stopped on the threshold of the room, his long, socked feet balanced between carpet and tile. "I have a one-cup-at-time maker, so it will take me a minute. Come sit down."

Lemon followed him into the open space and plunked into a wooden chair at the round kitchen table while George headed to the coffee maker.

Klee attempted to hoist himself into Lemon's lap on his own, only managing to catch his nails on her leggings and create a searing pain in her patella. She gave him a boost and waited him out while he turned in circles a few times seeking the perfect position on her lap. He'd just found his Zen spot when George spoke. "So do you still have Snickers?"

"Yes. He's staying with me for now. Poor little guy. I was at the search on Saturday."

George looked at her. "Oh yeah? You were there?"

Lemon nodded, keeping her focus on Klee.

"Did you all find anything?"

There hadn't been a single word in the media about the shoes, despite the coverage of the search over the weekend. Therefore Lemon wasn't sure if she was supposed to mention the shoes or not. Instead she shrugged.

George turned back to the coffee pot. "The antiquities curator, Ron, said they found something, but he didn't know what. Then they packed up yesterday but said they weren't done searching." He hit a button on the coffee machine and spun around, resting his hips against the counter. "Sometimes I wish they'd just say it straight, you know?"

"Yeah. I have no idea what to do. I mean, I still have a key to her place, and her dog, and I don't know what to do." Lemon shrugged again. She knew she was doing a crappy job of being a sneaky spy, but lying about the coffee was about as far as her nefarious skill set went.

George crossed his arms over his chest, the massive muscles bulging. "I know what you mean. Jillian was the president of the board. And I'm the vice president. I was supposed to take over as president in a year and half. But I guess I need to step up now. I mean, I realize there are bigger things at stake here, but I feel like…I don't know, like I deserve to know what's up."

Lemon had known that Jillian was the board president, but she had no idea George was her appointed successor. This knowledge combined with his need to know made Lemon wonder what all George had a stake in Jillian's death. "Yeah. That's a lot of pressure."

"Oh man. The texts have been non-stop. And the press is hounding us. Like we know anything. Go talk to the cops." He held out his hand. "We don't know anything."

"So, did you have a board meeting that day or something?" The question felt like a transparent dig for information, and Lemon nearly flinched as it left her mouth.

George, however, didn't seem to find it out of the ordinary at all. His expression remained the same. "On Thursday? No. We meet on Wednesdays. We'd actually had a meeting the day before she went missing."

"So, she was okay that day?"

"Sure. Her usual cantankerous self. Didn't you walk Snickers on Wednesday?"

Lemon nodded, her throat so dry she wasn't sure she'd be able to speak, but she managed to get her words out. "Yeah, but I didn't see her that day because she was out on meetings."

"Oh, sure, right. You walk that dog in the afternoon. Well, I saw her, and she was the same old Jillian, full of piss and vinegar."

Lemon was still formulating her next question, trying to pose it without raising suspicion, when George said, "Coffee's ready."

He filled her travel mug and held it out to her. Lemon placed Klee on the ground and stood, taking the cup. "Thank you so much. I will bring the mug back."

"No problem. I mean, I hate going out this early, that's why I hire you." He reached out and patted Klee's head. "Have fun buddy."

By the time Lemon had placed Klee in the back of the van with the other dogs, her certainty that his kind owner was completely innocent had waned.

CHAPTER SIX

Her usual bench seat was taken by a couple with a bouncy Frenchie Lemon had never seen before. Perching herself on a concrete wall instead, she watched as Klee attempted to make friends with the Bulldog. The other dogs were far less interested in operating outside their clique. They ignored the newcomer as well as the two regulars—an Italian Greyhound and an inexplicable Terrier mix—and chased each other in a deranged circle around the artificial turf, stopping only occasionally to get a sloppy drink of water from the bathtub-sized, communal dish.

The happy mutts didn't demand much of Lemon's attention, so she didn't feel bad about checking her phone when it vibrated in her pocket. Seeing that it was Mei, she immediately answered. "Hey."

"Good morning, sunshine."

"Aren't you at work?"

"Yeah. Aren't you?"

Lemon smiled to herself. "Yep. I'm going to guess that you are hiding in the catacombs somewhere?" Their nickname for the museum archives always gave Lemon the vision of a set of dark, stone tunnels jammed with artifacts despite the fact that Mei had assured her it was not at all what it looked like in real life.

"Yeah. I had to find out how it went with George."

Lemon took a measured breath. She wanted to relate her conversation with George in the most objective way possible. "He said that the board was kind of freaking out."

"Tell me about it. Everyone here is freaking out. Jillian's the board president."

"Yeah, he said that he's the vice president."

"Yeah."

"You didn't mention that."

"I didn't?"

"I would have remembered."

Mei relented. "Of course you would have. Yeah. He's the vice."

"He said it means he is, like, the next president."

"Yeah. That's how it works. There is technically a vote, but the vice is basically assumed to be the next prez."

Lemon shifted the phone from one ear to the other, her eyes tracking Mooney the chiweenie as she did. He was known for his libido, since he hadn't yet been fixed, and she wanted to keep him in check. "He said he basically had to take over now."

"Yeah, I guess he does. Oh, my God. It just hit me. Do you know what that means?"

"No. What?"

"He killed her."

Lemon nearly fell off the concrete wall. "What? Why?"

"To get the painting."

"What on earth are you talking about?"

"Okay, sorry." Mei took in a deep breath. "Let me start from the beginning."

"Please."

"Remember I said they were fighting over a painting?"

"Yeah. You mentioned it when we were at Jade's."

"So Ron found this absolutely incredible painting."

"Wait. Your boss, Ron? Milo's owner? I thought he was the curator for antiquities. You don't, like, have a lot of paintings." Lemon suddenly felt stupid. She'd been to the exhibit area Mei worked on, and while there weren't any of the traditional paintings that decorated the walls of the rest of the massive museum, there were plenty of things that had been *painted on.* "Oh wait. Like frescoes."

"No," Mei's voice rose in excitement. "That's just it. Ron found an *easel painting* from ancient Rome."

"Is that even a thing?"

"Not really. There are frescoes that show that easel paintings existed in ancient Rome, but no one has ever actually found one. And Ron did. This is a *huge* deal. And the Board voted to buy it, but Jillian voted not to, and even though she was overruled, she was still trying to stop the purchase."

Lemon scratched her head. "Still confused."

"So this painting is literally one of a kind, right? And it's going to cost the museum a pretty penny. But it will put the Legion, who some people say is the stepbrother of the California art scene, in a huge international spotlight. I mean, big, big deal. But Jillian was against buying the painting. George was totally for it. And for the last year she's been trying to stop the whole thing. During that time George managed to raise the money to buy it from a bunch of rich tech investors."

"Wait, he raised all the money?" Lemon asked.

"Yeah, and Jillian was *still* against buying the painting."

"Why?"

"Nobody knows. I mean, at least nobody who will talk to me about it knows. I'm sure George does, and probably the rest of the Board."

Lemon remembered Jillian's particular interest in ancient Rome. It even dominated the decorating theme in her apartment, from images of ancient aqueducts on the walls to coffee table books about Roman architecture lovingly placed on glass tables.

"It doesn't make sense," Lemon said. "She loved the museum and antiquities. I don't get it."

"Well, me neither. But that's all I know. She was blocking the painting's purchase. George wanted it bad. And now she's dead. He's in charge. And the deal will probably be done by the end of the week."

"People don't kill people over paintings."

"Oh, hell yes they do. Especially ones worth millions of dollars."

Lemon rubbed her right heel over the toe of her left shoe. She'd been loath to get involved in the amateur investigation when it was first discussed at Jade's place. Now she was contemplating immersing herself further in it. "Okay. So, you work this from your end. See what you can find out from the museum staff. And I'll try to probe George some more. We need to know why Jillian was against buying that painting."

"Yes! We are doing this." Mei's enthusiasm was loud, but it couldn't drown out Lemon's worry.

Snickers was a relatively good listener. All through making dinner, Snickers sat at the edge of the kitchen, his head cocked to one side, his eyes following Lemon's every move. He never once fled the conversation as Lemon ran down her anxiety over George.

"He's a really nice, guy, ya know. I mean, who runs around trying to trick a really nice guy into admitting to murder? And I don't care how much money was at stake, he's not going to *murder* anyone over it. Seriously. It just doesn't make sense. I mean, it's not like he's getting the money, right? Unless this art dealer is, like, his cousin or something and he gets a kickback."

She flipped her veggie burner in the pan and gazed at her fluffy counselor. "I mean, that seems unlikely, right?"

Snickers cocked his head the other direction.

"Sure, he'd lose a lose a little face with the donors if he talked it up and then couldn't make the deal happen. But he isn't going to *kill* someone over a little embarrassment."

Snickers huffed and laid his head on the ground. Apparently, he'd given up trying to make sense of Lemon's convoluted diatribe. Lemon turned back to her burger. It popped and sizzled and generally indicated it was nearly ready.

She'd just switched off the burner when her phone rang. Since all her frequent callers had their own special tones, the general ring usually meant a client calling to cancel or change their plans.

Lemon scooped up the phone and hit the answer button quickly. "Hello?"

"Is this Lemon?"

"Yeah. Hi." She glanced at the phone's screen but all that stared back at her was a string of numbers she didn't recognize.

"Hi. This is Mike Ross. Jillian's son."

Lemon was swamped with guilt. Jillian had given her Mike's number. He was the emergency contact for Snickers. Here it was Monday and she still hadn't called him. She just scooped up Jillian's dog and spirited him away to her apartment. "Oh Mike. I'm sorry I didn't call earlier."

"Oh. That's okay. I mean, I didn't really expect you to. But," Mike let out a long sigh. "The police have declared my mom dead, and so I am trying to wrap some things up."

"I'm sorry, Mike."

With the tone of a person practiced at fielding those words a million times over the last few days, Mike said, "Thank you. Yes. It's been hard, especially without knowing where she is or what happened."

Lemon swallowed back her own emotions, the ones she only poured into Snickers fur at night. If this was hard for her, it must be a nightmare for Mike. "I suppose you're calling about Snickers."

"Yes. I am."

Lemon's chest tightened. She knew she had no claim on Snickers, but she hated to give him up. There was a connection between them now. They'd been through this together, and now they were each other's comfort. She stared at the top of Snicker's head. "Yes. Of course. Do you want me to bring him to your house tonight or is tomorrow okay?"

"Oh, God no. Please don't bring him here."

Mike's reaction pulled Lemon out of her melancholy so fast she jerked her head back in shock.

"I mean," Mike said, his voice more tempered. "My wife is allergic. We don't actually want him. It's just that…well, my lawyer says that if he ends up in a shelter it will look bad. He seems to think it will end up in the news. You know, a sad, pathetic looking dog in a cage because Jillian's heartless son didn't want to take him in."

Mike Ross had gone from sympathetic mourner to narcissistic dog-hater faster than Snickers could wolf down a pup patty from the local burger joint. Lemon had no words. Her lack of ability to speak left a sickly static filling the phone line.

"So, do you still have him?" Mike asked.

"Yes."

"Do you know anyone who might want a dog?"

"Me," Lemon said quickly. "I'll keep him."

"Really? That's great. Thank you, Lemon."

"Yeah. No problem."

"You, you don't want any money or anything do you?"

Lemon's stomach churned. Something was deeply wrong here. "No. No. It's all good. If you don't mind, I'll just keep Snickers. I promise he won't end up in a shelter."

"Thanks. I appreciate it."

Snickers peeked up at her as the awkward quiet once again enfolded them. She winked at him. They *were* in this together. They were a team.

"Okay. Well, yeah, thanks, then."

"Sure. Take care Mike."

"Yep. You too. Bye."

Lemon, the phone still clutched in her hand, dropped to her knees and rubbed her face in Snicker's poofy fur. "You're all mine, sweetheart. I hope you don't mind."

Snickers rewarded her with a lick to the chin, which she took as confirmation of his acceptance. Lemon leaned back, sitting on her heels and wiped at her face. Now that Snicker's fate was sealed, there was something else that had to be dealt with.

That phone call with Mike crawled under Lemon's skin and planted itself in her mind. She wouldn't forget that call and the way it made her feel, ever. So she settled herself beside Snickers, her back resting against the oven door. With one hand tangled in Snicker's fur, she used the other to send a text to Mei and Jade in the group chat Mei had started and named "the Nancy Drews".

We need to look into Mike Ross.

CHAPTER SEVEN

There were a handful of times in Lemon's life when she could not pinpoint exactly why she was doing what she was doing. The first memory of such an incident was during a family trip. She was seven and her parents had decided they were all going to zipline down some insane forest canopy thing in Belize. Due to her small size and young age, she ended up strapped to her father staring down at the tops of leafy, green trees and wondering why the hell she had agreed to this.

The second memory was from high school. For some reason Lemon had allowed Mei to talk her into performing in the annual talent show as Laurel and Hardy. She stood on that stage, bathed in the hottest, brightest, light of all time. The damn spotlight, run by Lyka Smith, basically rivaled the sun. Sweat poured down her face as she donned a three-piece suit and attempted to remember the punch line to all the jokes. And all she could think the whole time was: why the hell did I agree to this.

Number three was in the making right here outside the Legion of Honor. This time she knew why she'd agreed to this crazy plan. Because Jade had suggested it. As hard as it was to admit that Jade's complex hazel eyes might have had something to do with her poor choices, it was the truth.

So here she was, one hand on Milo's leash, the other holding the rest of the afternoon crew. If she had time in the day to walk Milo separately, she might consider it, but a San Francisco dog walker had no choice but to walk as many dogs at once or risk not making enough money to pay the highly inflated bills that came with living in the city. As a result, Milo's nose, hard at work already, probed the ground, cataloging every miniscule smell while his companions tagged along, unknowing. Lemon hoped Milo did not succeed in the mission Jade set for him. She had no interest in finding the rest of Jillian.

But Jade was right. Milo had found her feet. And according to Jade, that meant he was capable of smelling cadavers. If the rest of Jillian's dead body was out here somewhere, Milo should be able to detect it.

The police had pulled up stakes behind the Legion of Honor the day before, convinced it would yield no more of Jillian than it already had. So, the area sat free and clear now. Jade wanted Milo's nose to give the place one more go round, and Lemon just couldn't bring herself to say no to the hot crime scene investigator.

Milo led the way across the stiff grass, winding through various-sized tree trunks dotting the slim tract of woods. The other dogs continually tried to pull Lemon in two by veering in the opposite direction of Milo's path. After the third time she'd nearly lost an arm, Lemon regrouped the dogs into one pack, giving Milo extra lead.

He moved out in front of the gang, his long ears dragging on the ground as his nose probed every nook and cranny of the wooded area as his short legs carried him along. The other dogs suddenly became overly curious about Milo's activities. Now they yanked at Lemon, straining to get involved.

Lemon attempted to pretend she actually wanted Milo to find something. She didn't know much about scent detection with dogs— okay she didn't know anything about it—but since Milo's great discovery everyone seemed to think of her as some sort of magical dog handler.

One thing she was certain about was that scent detection dog handling must involve more than simply willing the dog to find whatever you were looking for. Even if that methodology dominated the dog-training books, Lemon failed. She flinched every time Milo so much as paused his forward motion, terrified he would start digging again.

After a good thirty-minute sniff fest, the Basset Hound completed his task. He plopped on a thick patch of grass, stuck his tongue out and announced his intention not to move for a good, long while. The other dogs didn't fight it. Milo was their ruler, and they followed suit.

Lemon knew better than to try to oppose the will of the canine king and took a seat herself among the scattered dogs. She pulled her phone out of the pocket of her hoodie and opened the group chat for the Nancy Drews.

No body parts found. Milo's limited energy depleted.

It didn't take long for Jade's reply. *Damn. I had big hopes for that nose.*

As much as she feared a discovery, Lemon still felt a twinge of guilt that Milo didn't fulfill Jade's dreams. *Sorry. We can try again tomorrow.*

Cool, Mei texted back. *BTW we need to talk about the painting. Got more info. Dinner tonight?*

Then Jade texted, *How about that place next to Hillary's. Good hummus.*

Lemon bit her lip. Her checkbook felt a little tight these days since she was saving up money to change the horrible bright purple letters the size of Labrador Retrievers smeared across both sides of her van announcing Dilly's Doggos. *How about Chinese take-out at my place. Easier to talk.*

Good thinking, Jade replied.

See you then. Mei messaged, sealing the deal.

The paper bags rustled as Lemon pulled each carton out and placed it on the table. Mei rummaged through the kitchen drawers producing utensils and eco-friendly non-paper towels. Jade, intent on being helpful, ran the items Mei handed her over to the table and set three places. Snickers followed her.

"Pretty sure that dog is in love you," Mei said.

After dropping the last fork into place, Jade stared down at the dog. "The feeling is mutual." She bent and gave Snickers a good scratch behind the ears. "No matter how much I begged as a kid, my parents never let me have a dog. My brother was allergic. I'd be lying if I didn't admit that I despised him just a little bit for that."

"Snickers is hypo-allergenic," Lemon said.

"Of course you are, you sweet little thing." Jade dropped to her knees and pressed her face into Snicker's, receiving several enthusiastic kisses in return. The evidence that Jade was a dog lover made Lemon's libido leap into the air.

"What are we drinking?" Mei asked.

"Depends." Lemon opened the last carton, revealing a gorgeous pile of General Tso's chicken. "Do we need to be sober for this conversation?"

Jade looked up from Snickers. "Absolutely not."

Mei swung around the corner of the island. "No way."

"I have a bottle of Syrah and a bottle of Sake. Take your pick," Lemon said.

"Are they both in the usual spot?"

"Yep." Lemon didn't bother to point to the cupboard. Mei knew. Instead she folded up the paper bags into a neat pile and carried them to the recycle bin.

Mei asked, "What do you want, Jade?"

Jade shifted from her knees to sitting cross-legged beside Snickers on the floor. She rested back on her arms and chewed on her bottom lip. Jade gazed up at the ceiling as she contemplated her choices. "Hmmmm." The long, low sound vibrating through the room created an unnamed sensation traveling through Lemon's body. "Sake sounds like a fun treat."

"I should have gotten sushi instead of Chinese," Lemon said, even though she knew sushi was beyond what her bank account could handle.

Jade smiled up at her. "Next time."

Lemon turned away, unwilling to let Jade see whatever expression of blatant lust painted her face. "Yeah, for sure."

Mei poured the Sake, along with large glasses of water. They took their places at the island and filled their plates. Conversation lulled, and eventually, the eating slowed. Tummies filled up. One-by-one they abandoned their plates and leaned back, little cups of Sake in hand. Slowly, the discussion returned.

"We have to look at George Nichols," Mei said. "He had the motive. And probably the opportunity. I mean, he could get Jillian to an early morning meeting, right? They are president and vice president of the board."

"So, what?" Jade asked. "He lures her to a meeting at the museum and kills her there. How does he cut off her feet at the museum and leave no trace?"

Mei raised a hand in the air. "Maybe he killed her and cut off her feet outside the museum."

"How would no see that?" Lemon asked. "I mean, that's just implausible."

"He killed her somewhere else. His house maybe."

Jade jumped in with a question of her own. "Why dump her feet outside the museum?"

Mei rubbed her chin between her thumb and forefinger. "To send a message?"

"This is not a mob movie," Lemon said. "Besides, I don't think George did it. And I've been in his house. It didn't look like a crime scene to me, or like it had recently been cleaned."

"Cutting off body parts is messy," Jade said.

Mei pointed her finger at Lemon. "Yeah, but did you look in his bathtub?"

Not interested in the image that formed behind her eyelids, Lemon turned the conversation in a different direction. "I just don't see the motive for George to *murder* someone."

Jade leaned forward, her elbows braced on the table. "Tell us more about this painting situation, Mei."

Mei matched Jade's position across the table and plunged into the conversation with enthusiasm. "My boss, Ron, found this one-of-a-kind, totally priceless, absolutely knock-the-socks-off-the-art-world incredible piece. He went to the Board and told them all about it. This was, like, a couple months before I started. And they needed to come up with twenty-five million dollars to purchase it for the museum. Which, honestly, is a bit of a bargain for this. The dealer hadn't talked to any other museums. This is big deal."

"Okay, but, it's not like George is going to get the painting and hang it up in his living room," Lemon said.

"No. But it's his legacy," Mei said. "He went to everyone he knows and raised that money on the promise that it would hang in the museum and the whole world would come to see it."

"He just doesn't strike me as someone who cares about things like that," Lemon said.

Mei rolled her eyes. "Why, because he has a little dog that he treats like a royal prince?"

The answer to that was emphatically yes, but Lemon felt stupid saying it now. She wasn't sure where to go from here.

"Okay," Jade said. "So, Jillian didn't want to buy this painting even though George raised all the money for it? Also, where the hell does twenty-five million come from?"

"Please. Have you been to SOMA lately?" Mei quirked up one side of her mouth. "The tech industry, baby." She rubbed her fingers together.

"But, yeah. I mean, Jillian couldn't really stop the purchase all by herself, could she? Not if the rest of the board wanted it. It's like a democracy, isn't it?"

"Technically, yes." Mei said. "But from what I hear, Jillian is pow-er-ful. If she wants something—or doesn't want something—she will get her way. She can lobby other people, talk to donors. I don't know. All I know is that word around the museum is, 'don't cross Jillian.' Because you *will* lose."

"So, speaking of which," Lemon said. "What about Mike and Tina?

I mean, I talked to Mike and it did not seem like there was any love lost in that relationship. And you were supposed to ambush Tina while she got her nails done, Mei. How did that go?"

Mei leaned back and took a sip of her drink. "I got nothing. I brought up Jillian, and every time I did, she changed the subject. Which my aunt said was weird because she bitches about Jillian on the regular during her appointments."

"Well, what *did* she talk about?" Jade asked.

Mei threw her hands in the air. "Oh God. She talked about Mike and how he doesn't work out as much as he used to, and he's not as hot as he was when she married him. She talked about her sister's cousin who recently got out of a cult and is going to be on a podcast about it. And her nails. Lots about her nails."

"Did she say anything about money?" Lemon asked. "I mean, Mike is about to inherit a lot of it. Or so I would assume."

"Nope. Not a word.

"What if he isn't going to inherit it." Jade said.

Lemon glanced at Jade, her cheek resting on her fist. "What do you mean?"

Jade leaned forward. "I don't know. What if Jillian disinherited Mike or was about to and he had to off her before she changed the will. That's a motive all the time."

Mei held up one finger "Sure. On T.V."

Lemon's need to defend Jade rose to the surface. "You're one to talk. Your motive is straight out of Columbo."

That little dig started a round of laughing. It felt good to Lemon to finally experience a little mirth, something absent in her life since Milo found Jillian's foot buried in the soil beneath a Eucalyptus tree.

Mei turned her gaze on Jade. "You know, the whole 'Jillian is a hard ass' thing my co-workers were telling me made me wonder about Hayley."

Jade sat back and frowned. "I wish I could tell you something. But Hayley seems to be avoiding me. I've tried calling, texting, and even

DMs. I'm getting nothing."

"Hmmmmm." Mei's little hum was far more accusatory than its innocent single syllable might indicate.

"We can't really think Hayley murdered someone though, right?"

"Lemon, you always think the best of people." Mei said. "It's…"

Jade jumped in to finish the thought. "I think it's sweet."

Lemon met Jade's intense gaze, their eyes locking together. Her leg started to bounce on its own, hidden by the small table. She clutched her jeans in her fist, creating a ball of wrinkled denim. "Thanks."

"Shit."

Lemon ripped her gaze away from Jade to peer over at Mei who was holding her phone up to her face. "What's up?"

"My grandmother. She's headed back to the hospital." Mei rose. "I gotta go."

Lemon jumped up as well. "You want me to come with you?"

"No. It's okay. We'll just sit in the emergency room waiting for a few hours until they get her sugar under control and then send her home."

"You sure?"

Mei smiled and kissed Lemon on the cheek. "I'm sure. I'll call you when I get bored." Her eyes darted between Lemon and Jade. "Stay here and solve the murder mystery, and, um, have fun."

After walking Mei to the door, Lemon spun around to find Jade standing near the kitchen table, an expression of empathy on her face. The way her eyes shone and her mouth dipped down just a tiny bit at the corners drew Lemon toward her.

Without any real cognition, Lemon moved to stand directly in front of Jade, staring up at her, knowing that her face must be reflecting the pleading inside. She placed one hand on Jade's hip. Jade responded by moving closer. She leaned down and slowly pressed her lips against Lemon's, creating a burst of desire that hit Lemon with the force of six dogs dragging her toward a side of beef.

CHAPTER EIGHT

Wednesdays exhausted Lemon. She managed to walk ten miles and wrangle fifteen dogs over a nine-hour period each day. Taking one day at a time was the best method of survival over the course of the week. But for some reason, she could never do that on Wednesdays. It always felt like she was halfway up the mountain and had run out of oxygen.

Not even that amazing kiss from last night kept her bolstered after the coffee crew spilled her morning elixir all over her and the mid-day crew made her late for the afternoon crew because Milo insisted on taking a long nap under the dome at the Palace of Fine Arts, and he convinced everyone else to do that same. It took a handful of treats and a lot of coaxing to get them all up and moving again.

She managed to grab all the afternoon dogs and get them to the dog park before sunset threatened, but dark crept in by the time she dropped off the last of her charges. Tilly played hard at the park, and Lemon had to carry her up the concrete stairs to Nancy's front door.

Nancy greeted them with a wide smile. "My precious," she squealed, reaching for a squirming Tilly. Lemon deposited Tilly into Nancy's arms and followed her into the house. With a brief stop at the tall glass jar perched on a credenza so Nancy could pluck a dog treat out and give it to a wide-eyed Tilly, they settled into the living room.

"How's Snickers?" Nancy asked while her chin was actively being licked by Tilly's tiny tongue.

"He's good. Happy boy. He gets to come on walks whenever He wants, stay home when he's feeling lazy, like today." She smiled, unable to keep the happiness she felt as a new dog owner from showing on her face.

"I'm glad he has you. The idea of him living with Mike and that Tina makes me sick. Tina'd probably beat the poor thing."

"I don't think they'd keep him," Lemon said, remembering her conversation with Mike. He'd been pretty clear that if it were up to him and his wife Snickers would be in a shelter.

Nancy's mouth dropped open. "Monsters."

"I'd rather he be up for adoption than abused."

"Either one is unacceptable."

Lemon decided to shift the conversation. "Tell me about Mike and Jillian. He was an only child, right? And Jillian was divorced?"

"Yeah, he was an only child. His mom and dad's marriage was shit. But they stayed together for him. When they divorced, the jackass took off to Europe. Mike never really got over it. Blamed Jillian for running his dad off."

"That sounds hard." Lemon had been blessed with parents who stayed married and made it through all the rough times. But she had plenty of friends whose parents didn't make it. And as a fellow only child, she couldn't begin to image the strain when the two people who were your whole world split.

"Oh, it was. Jillian tried very hard to keep Mike happy."

"And now?"

"Things are…strained. When Mike graduated from college, he interviewed for a job at the family company. Jillian was the CEO then. Her father started Noth, Inc. back when tech meant room-sized computers. So young, naïve, Mike applied for an executive position when he was fresh out of college. Instead, he got a mailroom job. He worked his way up to middle management, but not without a lot of whining. And it got worse when he married Tina."

"Why?"

"Well, for starters, Jillian didn't approve of the marriage. Not at all. She thought Tina wasn't good enough for Mike. And she was too young. They didn't get along from day one. And then there was the money issue."

"What's that?"

Nancy leaned toward Lemon. "Tina isn't satisfied with Mike's salary. And Mike only has a handful of company shares he inherited from his grandfather. Even if he were to sell them, they wouldn't amount to much. And Tina didn't like that. According to Jillian, Tina only married Mike for his money. And when she discovered he wasn't worth that much, she was disappointed. She basically started a campaign to get Mike the money she thought was rightfully theirs."

"That's intense."

"It gets worse. She once told Mike—in a room in Jillian's house where she thought they were alone—that Mike needed to ask for the money now and not worry about what would happen later. According to Jillian, she said, 'You're going to get the money anyway when she dies. Why wait.' Jillian was *pissed*."

"I can imagine," Lemon said.

"Jillian told me she threatened Mike."

"Threatened him how?"

"She told him if he didn't get a hold on his wife she'd cut him out of her will."

Lemon's head snapped back. A niggling sensation crawled up her spine. She flashed back to Jade's television-based theory. "When was this?"

Nancy waved her hand and dropped back into the couch. "A while back. I don't remember exactly when. But I can tell you he took the threat seriously. He must have. Those two live well above their means. He's mid-level in the company, and she doesn't work at all, and they spend like they've got money to burn. They both drive expensive cars. They live in a fancy condo. It just doesn't add up."

Lemon and Nancy held each other's gaze for a long beat. The

moment lasted a near eternity. Unable to move, Lemon merely held eye contact.

Then Nancy suddenly shifted. Before Lemon could even comprehend what was happening, she grabbed her phone off the side table and quickly hit a contact before pressing the phone to her ear. The pause while Nancy waited for someone to answer gave Lemon the chance to assess what was happening, but it didn't help.

"Hi, Mike, it's Nancy. It's nice to hear your voice as well. How are you?"

Another long pause followed as Lemon strained to hear any scrap of information from the phone's receiver.

"Oh, I'm all right, I suppose. It's hard, you know." The beat of silence this time was shorter. Nancy said, "I wondered if you and Tina would like to have dinner with me and a few friends. You know I love dinner parties. It cheers me up a great deal." After another brief moment she said, "Excellent. How about Friday?" Then, "Great! We'll see you and your lovely wife then."

When Nancy hung up, she grinned at Lemon. "There. Now we can dig a little deeper, eh?"

Lemon nodded. "Can I bring some friends?"

Lemon enjoyed nachos as a common go-to for a mid-week dinner. Enhanced with homemade salsa, Mei appreciated it with a dramatic flourish. After a series of loud mmmmms, she proclaimed, "I swear, my mother will spend hours cooking and this took you twenty minutes and is just as good." Mei crammed another loaded chip into her mouth.

"I love you, Mei, but you really need to learn to fend for yourself. Only a few years until you're off your parents' insurance."

Mei rolled her eyes. "I get insurance with my job you know. I'll be okay."

Lemon dipped a chip in salsa and held it up. "You know what I mean."

"Okay, yeah. The deadline for adulting approaches. I've been thinking about that lately."

As Lemon munched, she considered their pact. The day they graduated college and moved back in with their parents, they both agreed it would only be temporary. They'd be on their own by the time they hit twenty-six. But it wasn't the easiest thing to do in a city with sky-high rents.

What Lemon often considered a hardship, her parents' sudden escape to Belize, was actually the luckiest of nudges. Her parents didn't just force their baby bird to fly, they gave her the means to do it. She needed to spread that wealth.

"Move in with me."

Mei chuckled. She held up her fingers, ticking them off one at a time. "This is the fourth time you've asked me."

"Imagine the level of rejection I'm feeling."

Mei gathered all the tiny tortilla chip crumbs in a pile in the center of her plate. "You know damn well I'd love that."

They didn't speak about the barrier they both knew prevented their plan from being achievable. Instead, Mei grinned. "Remember my condition though. We can't have a dog."

"Too bad. I have a dog."

They both glanced toward Snickers. His ears perked up at the attention and he lifted his head to stare at the humans.

Mei's face softened. "I have to admit, he's pretty damn cute."

"He's a good boy."

Mei left her seat and tentatively approached the pooch. She kneeled down in front of Snickers, who lifted his head slowly. Mei reached out her hand. The slight shaking was barely noticeable. Lemon stayed silent as Mei made peace with her fears. Snickers cooperated completely. He stretched his neck toward Mei in a quiet, careful move. Eventually, Mei's fingers landed on Snickers' right ear for a deep, satisfying scratch. After they had their moment, Mei looked up at Lemon. "You gotta take him to my Uncle Tom's studio on Saturday."

Tom might have been related to Mei through marriage, but he was one of her favorites. Lemon, too, enjoyed the eccentric photographer. After marrying Mei's aunt he opened a studio where he made a living taking portraits. On Saturdays he did pet portraits and all the proceeds went to the local shelter. People brought their animals down, dressed them up in capes and tiaras and let Tom do his magic.

"I do. I definitely do. We'll go this weekend."

"If you do it, I'll volunteer." Mei's uncle had been asking her to help him out on pet portrait day for months. He believed it would help her get over her fear of dogs. Mei said she never felt ready. But now, with Snickers' help, she'd clearly had a breakthrough. "Let's do it! Oh, and that is the day after the dinner with the potential killers. Did you ask Jade to that yet?"

"I literally got the invite from Nancy three hours ago."

"Call her now."

Lemon slowly reached out and palmed the phone. "I'll text her."

"Coward."

Lemon threw Mei a dirty look before typing up a text to Jade. *Nancy invited Mike and Tina Ross over to dinner on Friday night. Do you want to come?*

She took three deep, steady breaths as she penetrated the screen with her gaze, waiting for a reply.

Hell yes!

"She's coming," Lemon told Mei.

"I could tell by the goofy grin on your face."

"Shut up."

"Speaking of which, what happened between you two after I left the other night?"

Lemon knew the moment she'd sent Mei a string of heart emojis just after Jade left that she owed her best friend a story. But it didn't stop the warmth from crawling up her neck, just as it did every time she talked about a love interest since her first crush on Michael Nott in fourth grade.

"We kissed. Short and sweet. Nothing special." That was a lie, but one she could justify. It *was* short and sweet, and if it hadn't been for the massive electrical current that surged through her body during that brief touch of the lips, it probably wouldn't have been anything special.

"What happened after that? Did she take off?"

"No, she stayed for a while, we had another glass of wine and we talked."

"What did you talk about?"

"Books."

"Seriously? Books." Mei couldn't have looked more disappointed if she just heard she needed a root canal.

Lemon smiled and swung her feet beneath the barstool. "What can I say, we nerds get each other."

Lemon prided herself in her ability to balance a cup of coffee high above her shoulder in one hand and the phone in the other while the paws of a German Shepard hit her chest with loving enthusiasm. Once the dog ran off, a yappy Yorkie mix nipping at his heels, she lowered the cup and examined it. "Not a drop."

"What?"

"Nothing, Mom. What were you saying?"

"Are you at the dog park again?"

"Yeah. Of course."

"On a Saturday?"

"Mom, it's Thursday. Retirement's been good to you, I guess."

Her mother chuckled. "I teach two Yoga classes a week, you know."

"Mmmm Hmmm."

"So, Jillian. I was saying that Kelly McMann told Madge that they still haven't found the rest of her body."

"Not that I know of."

"Well, according to Kelly there's a rumor going around town that her body was dumped in the Bay. And the killer wasn't some dummy who did it wrong so she'll float into shore. No, this was a professional and she'll never be found."

Lemon took a sip of her coffee and savored the flavor before asking what she thought was an incredibly obvious question. "And how would anyone know that? Unless Kelly McMann is the killer, of course."

"Don't be ridiculous, Lemon. She just knows things."

Lemon contemplated trying to explain to her mother the absolute lack of logic involved in believing the twisted plot of a *Dateline* episode without a shred of evidence. Sure, that wouldn't get her anywhere, she just asked more questions. "Okay. But why cut off her feet?"

Certainty was clear in her voice as she said, "It's a warning."

"What kind of warning?"

"We've been mulling that over. I mean, where the feet were found certainly implies that the murder had something to do with the museum."

"And do you believe that. I mean, you knew Jillian, right?"

"Yeah. Didn't I tell you that?"

Lemon gave Tilly a pat and took another sip of coffee. "Yes, but you didn't tell me *how* you know her."

"Well back in the day, when you were little, me, Madge, Nancy, and Jillian were all on the same committee in the women's leadership group I belonged to."

"Wait. The women's leadership group?" Lemon remembered the organization. It still existed, in fact, and had grown quite large. Lemon's mother was still mentioned as part of the early days of the group and one of the people who had made it so successful. But something about that didn't compute. "Why was Nancy in it?"

"Oh honey, Nancy may not have had traditional jobs, but she was big on community service. She's been on just about every board there is to be on in San Francisco. Did you know she was the president of the Legion's board at one point?"

Lemon's spine straightened. "No, I didn't. When was this?"

"Oh, not long ago. Just before Jillian became president."

"So, wait. Nancy was the last board president before Jillian?"

"Yes. So?"

Lemon wasn't entirely sure why this tidbit of information was interesting to her, only that it piqued some inexplicable interest. "I don't know. It seems like a conflict of interest to have best friends back-to-back on the board."

"Well, it might be if their philosophy on art wasn't vastly different."

"What do you mean?" Lemon asked.

"I should think it'd be obvious. You've been in both their houses, right?"

"I mean, yeah? I know Jillian really likes antiquities and stuff."

"That's an understatement. And Nancy, she's into 19th Century art."

"Is that really that much of a difference?"

Her mother scoffed. "Well, it was to them. Friends or not, I witnessed some serious rows over art."

"Honestly, mom, that seems like a pretty silly thing to fight over."

Her mother clicked her tongue. "Lemon, sweetheart, you'd be surprised what rich and powerful people will argue over."

Lemon's mind drifted into dark, shadowy corners she had no intention of exploring. Every drop of information she gained over the last few days made her question all that she thought she knew.

CHAPTER NINE

With just twenty-four hours to go before they attended Nancy's sleuthing dinner party, Lemon kicked herself for not canceling on the invite to the Lu family dinner. She and Mei needed more time to plan, instead they were working another plot altogether.

"I have news," Mei announced. She raised her glass. That it contained only diet soda didn't seem to bother anyone. But neither of her parents, nor her teenaged brother moved to join their glass to hers. Only Lemon greeted her from across the table with her own glass of water.

Mei laughed and put down her drink. "I'm moving in with Lemon!"

The silence that blanketed the room lasted as long as it took Lemon to finish her soup. Then Mei's father broke it. "No. I don't think that's a good idea."

Mei's response was immediate and intense. "Dad, I am an adult!"

"I realize that," her father said, his voice calm and smooth.

"I can move out if I want."

"Nope. Not now."

Before Mei could protest further, her mother spoke. "In fact, perhaps Lemon should move in with us."

"What?" Mei's brother asked. "Where is she going to stay, exactly. With *her dog.*"

"Hush, Park," Mei's father said. "That's not the issue."

Mei leaned toward her dad. "What, exactly, *is* the issue?"

Mei's mother put her hand over Mei's. "This murder. We're worried about it. What if they are after you because you work at the museum, or Lemon because she found the…body parts?"

"Mom, no one is *after* us."

"You don't know that," her father said. "You don't know who killed Jillian or why, so how can you possibly be certain that you aren't in danger."

Mei turned her head away from her parents to meet Lemon's gaze with her own. With no answers to give, Lemon lifted her shoulders the tiniest bit. Mei swung her attention back to her parents. "We think we know who did it and why."

Lemon's knee bounced under the table the way it always had when Mei told a lie to her parents so they wouldn't get in trouble for some youthful exploit. She pressed her lips together as if she were trying to seal them.

"Mike and Tina Ross are the killers," Mei said. "They did it to get their inheritance."

Mei's father narrowed his eyes. "And how, exactly, do you know this?"

"We don't have proof just yet, but we're pretty sure."

"When they are in police custody you come talk to me about knowing who did it. In the meantime, you stay under this roof."

Under the table, Jade's knee brushed Lemon's. Lemon straightened and kept her focus on Mike. Thanks to Nancy's careful planning, Mike sat directly across the polished oval table from Lemon, while Tina sat across from Jade. Mei and Nancy flanked them at the ends.

"How's Snickers?" Mike's eyes softened as one hand reached down to stroke Tilly's fur.

Perhaps Mike's heart wasn't as cold as Lemon thought. "He's good. I mean, I'm sure he misses Jillian, but I got some of his stuff, like his bed and his favorite toys and moved them to my house to make him more comfortable.”

“That’s good,” Mike said. “I wasn’t sure if the police would let you in. They haven’t let me into mom’s house yet.”

Nancy leaned forward, her glass of wine hanging in her hand. “I made them retrieve all the items Lemon asked for and bring them to me.” She grinned, pride etched on her face. “And they did.”

“Good. I’m glad Snickers is being taken care of.”

“I think it’s ridiculous,” Tina said. “Her own son can’t get into her house but the stupid dog can have her stupid toys.”

Nancy set her glass carefully in front of her, the bottom clinking on the wood. Her hands moved to the edge of the table, gripping it so hard her knuckles turned white. “That dog—*he* by the way—was Jillian’s baby. He deserves to be comforted after losing his mommy.”

“What about the *human* who lost *his* mom?” Tina’s brown waves shook around her head as she thrust her thumb in Mike’s direction.

Mike’s voice was soft and weak. “Tina, it’s okay.”

“Hey Mike,” Jade’s words echoed through the room, drawing everyone’s attention. “I heard you got a promotion recently. Read it in SF Gate.”

Mike’s shoulders slumped and a soft smile painted his lips. “Yeah. I did, actually. I’m head of outside sales now.”

Nancy raised her glass of red wine. “Congratulations! To Mike’s promotion!” Her glass was quickly met with several others clinking together. Only Tina’s remained conspicuously absent from the toast.

“He should be CEO by now,” Tina said. “If his own mother hadn’t screwed him over.”

This subject piqued the interest of the people in the room with the objective of investigating the nature of Mike’s relationship with his mother. With four shocked expressions, anyone could have spoken first, but Mei beat them to the punch. “What do you mean by that?”

Mike recoiled from the table, tucking his body into the spindly wooden chair that perfectly matched the rest of Nancy’s dining set. Tina leaned forward, elbows against the table. "Mike should have been the CEO when his mother retired."

"I didn't have the experience," Mike said.

"Okay, well, you at least shouldn't have started in the fucking mail room. Your grandfather founded that company. But your mom sent you to the fucking bottom when you got out of college."

"And you worked your way up." Nancy raised her glass again. "Amazing!"

Mike's mouth formed a crooked line that reminded Lemon of the zig zag Charlie Brown face.

Tina spoke for him. "And now the company is run by this nightmare woman, Leslie Nygaard. She's completely unqualified and totally incompetent."

"But she *did* give Mike a promotion, right?" Nancy said. Tina shot Nancy a glare that could maim a lesser person. Nancy smirked. "Just saying."

But Tina wasn't having it. "The only reason Jillian made her the CEO when she left instead of Mike was because she's a woman. Jillian was such a rabid feminist she wishes she'd had a daughter instead of a son,"

Mike blanched. Lemon's heart thumped in empathy for him.

"I am telling you all." Tina pointed her finger at each person around the table. "That woman was a terrible mother."

"Mike, do you like art, too?" Mei blurted out.

Mike froze for a minute. "Yeah."

Mei leaned toward him, avoiding Tina's glare. "I mean, your mom was such a well-known art lover, I wondered if she passed that on to you."

Tina leaned back in her seat. Mike moved forward again, a seesaw of human motion. "She sure did."

"I'm an assistant curator at the Legion," Mei told him. "I work in the antiquities department."

"Near and dear to my mother's heart," Mike said. Unexpectedly he added, "And she passed that passion on to me."

"Oh yeah," Mei cocked her head. "You're an ancient art junkie, too?"

His mouth folded up in a subtle smile. "My favorites are roman frescoes. You?"

"Oh for sure. Magic on stone. Incredible," Mei said.

"I hate to interrupt this little art love fest," Nancy said. "But I have a question."

Mei and Mike both turned to Nancy, curiosity on their faces. Tina, on the other hand, wore an expression of fierce irritation.

"But, do you know anything about the Roman easel piece, Mike?"

"Mom and I never discussed it," he said. "But I heard about it from Ron."

"Ron, my boss, Ron?" Mei asked.

"Yes," Mike said. "He talked me into donating to the acquisition fund. It's very exciting, isn't it?"

Mei nodded. Tina rolled her eyes.

"George tried to get me to donate to that fund," Nancy said. "I turned him down. Sounded like BS to me."

Mike folded his arms over his chest. "It's the most exciting find in art history."

Nancy took a long sip of her wine. "We'll see. An undiscovered Monet, now that would be something."

Mike chuckled. "You never change, Nancy."

"Nope."

"I do wish mom would have kept her promise about the museum board, though." Mike's voice dripped regret.

Lemon's curiosity broke through her proclivity to let Mei do all the talking. "What promise?"

Mike's blue eyes, eyes that looked so much like his mother's, met hers. "She said she'd get me elected to the Legion board before her term as president was up. I don't care if it's considered nepotism. I wanted it badly. I believed her when she promised it to me. And maybe it would have happened. I don't know. Her term was almost up, though. And she hadn't done it yet. I have to wonder if she ever would have."

"I bet she would've," Lemon said. "She was such a kind a person."

Mike's eyes were glued to her face. Tina's glare, on the other hand, was like a bullet ramming into the side of her head.

"Thanks, Lemon," Mike said.

"What a laugh," Tina said. "She was a total bitch."

Nancy narrowed her eyes at Tina, her lips pressed together in a hard line.

Mike cleared his throat and glanced at his phone. "Got an emergency call." He stood abruptly, causing the glasses on the table to wobble ominously. "We have to go." He wrapped his hand around Tina's upper arm and pulled her to a standing position beside him. "It's an emergency."

Before they could get anymore incriminating information from either of the Ross's, they were gone.

"Let me get that for you." Jade took control of the wine opener as Lemon moved out of the way.

"Thanks," Lemon slid along the counter toward the frosted glass cabinet that held her mother's fancier dishes. She pulled three delicate wine glasses out and snagged a few of the cute little wire markers tucked in a wooden box no bigger than what would hold a necklace.

"Oh my God, your mom's wine charms!" Mei reached over the island as Lemon approached. She clamped her fingers and thumb like a baby shark chomping its prey. "I want to see my choices."

Lemon placed her hand, palm up, on top of the counter. The cork popped beside her, causing her to jump. Jade smiled and set the bottle, now freed from its stopper, on the counter before leaning over to examine the objects in Lemon's hand.

Mei pushed the three charms around with her finger before plucking one up. "I want the Scottie dog."

Lemon moved her hand closer to Jade, offering up her wares. "Which one do you want?"

"These go on your wine glass so you know which is which?" Jade asked.

Lemon grinned. "Yeah. Silly, but fun. My mom got them as a gift from her best friend Madge, which is the same person who left me the dog-walking business. I guess it's appropriate that they're all dogs."

Jade gently pulled the charm featuring a tiny, silver Beagle from Lemon's hand. It dangled between her fingers as she grinned at it. "I never thought I would be enamored with something so cheesy."

"Wait till you meet my mom," Lemon said. As soon as the words were out of her mouth she sank away from the counter and escaped to the other side of the room in the guise of retrieving the remaining wine glasses. Talking about meeting her mother to a woman she'd kissed exactly once created a wave of embarrassment she had no choice but to ride out.

"How about that Nancy," Mei said, saving Lemon with a change of subject.

"She's something all right." Jade poured wine into the first glass then slid it over to Mei. When Lemon returned with the other two, she pulled them out of her hands. "Glad she's on our side."

Lemon slid into the bar stool beside Mei and accepted the glass Jade handed her. Jade remained standing opposite them both. "To Nancy," she said, raising her glass.

Lemon and Mei met her toast. The obligatory sip following the toast led right back into the conversation. "Do you really think Nancy suspects Mike and Tina?" Mei asked.

Lemon shrugged. "The dinner party was her idea. And she's known Mike all his life."

"I'm not sure Mike is a good suspect. That guy doesn't have a killer feel," Jade said.

Lemon nearly leapt over the counter to hug her. "I totally agree. He seems sad about his mom. And sort of…weak."

"His wife, on the other hand," Mei said. "Is straight out of a TV special. That chick is e-vil."

"And she totally has her thumb on him," Jade said. "If she wanted him to do something—say like hide a body—he would do it. Guaranteed."

"And he'd feel bad about it," Lemon said.

"Maybe," Jade said. "But I want to know what was in his bag."

"Wait. What are you talking about?" Mei asked.

Jade bent at the waist, leaning her entire torso over the counter. "When we came into Nancy's, Mike and Tina were already there, right?"

"Yeah, so?" Mei asked.

"So, I was first in the door and you guys might not have seen, but as we walked in, Mike was stuffing papers into that messenger bag hanging off his chair."

Lemon remembered the drab, green bag. Slung over the knob of his chair, it hung there, protected by Mike's body throughout the dinner. When he and Tina got up to leave, he immediately clutched it to his chest. Lemon's interest in what lay inside ramped up significantly with Jade's reveal.

"Do we think Nancy saw these papers?" Mei asked.

"I mean, I assume she did. It's not like he's going to secretly spread them out on her table without her knowing."

Lemon spun the stem of her wine glass in her fingers. "But Nancy didn't mention it to us after they left."

"No, she didn't," Jade agreed.

"Well, that's it then." Mei slammed her hand on the counter, sending a shock through Lemon. "We have to find out what's in that bag."

"And how, exactly, are we going to do that?" Lemon asked.

A mischievous grin spread across Mei's face. She stared straight at Snickers, who lay leisurely on the floor at the edge of the kitchen, his head resting on his paws. "*He's* going to do it," she said, pointing in the dog's direction.

CHAPTER TEN

The diverse barking—from high pitched and constant to low and occasional—greeted Lemon as soon as she stepped through the door of Mei's Uncle Tom's studio. Despite being crammed with animals and their human companions, the foyer was surprisingly well organized. One very firm line, flanked by a steel and fabric barrier that prevented all species from leaving the tight space, stretched into the main room of the studio. A second line guided a faster moving group pouring out of the studio.

Lemon knew that Snickers, who'd grown accustomed to ignoring other dogs thanks to all his time with Lemon and the various packs she walked, generally ignored all non-human animals. Here his focus remained fixed on the people, Lemon assumed it was because he thought those were the creatures who might possibly have cookies in their pockets. Based on the way Snicker's nose reached toward the light brown purse carried by the person with the Pug near the front of the line it was apparent to Lemon that the woman clearly stashed goodies in there.

Even as the line moved forward and the woman with the treats moved into the studio and out of sight, Snickers was on the move, straining at the end of the leash and causing an ache in Lemon's shoulder until she finally had to scoop up the pup. The line moved forward and Snicker's head drooped onto Lemon's arm, his fuzzy chin fully dependent on

Lemon to keep it from becoming victim to gravity.

By the time her turn finally arrived, Lemon's feet hurt from standing on the hard linoleum floor. Mei slid open a black velvet curtain. The sound of the metal rings rubbing against the wooden dowel holding up the makeshift barrier caused Snickers to stir in Lemon's arms.

"Are you ready for your close-up, my dears?" The top hat perched on Mei's head slid to the side. The tiny dogs scattered across its fabric seemed to dance.

"Yep. We gave our donation to Lynn."

Mei smiled coyly. Her crush on the shelter manager, Lynn, was a well-guarded secret. Lemon suspected that wanting to spend time with Lynn had more to do with Mei's volunteerism than her desire to get over her fear—which appeared to be in check at the moment. "Right this way."

Mei held out her arm and Lemon scooted into a spacious studio. Cameras and lights took up the space opposite a broad wall with changeable backgrounds. Various seats and props littered the open space and a shelf with doggie toys and treats was tucked in one corner.

"We're doing a walk in the woods today." Mei pointed to the realistic-looking canvas backdrop.

"Lovely," Lemon said.

"Hi, Lemon." Tom waved at her from behind the camera.

Lemon waved back at his silhouette as the bright lights obscured her vision.

"Cute dog," Tom said. "We have some bright leashes to use."

"Wait. I'm going to be in the picture?"

"Of course," Mei said. "That's the idea. It's a family portrait."

Lemon had pictured an adorable image of Snickers in a funny hat, not something involving her own mug. "I'm…"

"Perfect," Mei said, brushing a lock of hair off Lemon's forehead. "You look great." She shoved Lemon into place and slapped a bright turquoise leash in her hand.

A few treats, toy squeaks, and difficult to follow instructions later,

Tom had taken a handful of shots and Mei ushered Lemon and Snickers out the door with a kiss on each of Lemon's cheeks. "See you on Monday."

Still blinking her eyes from the flashes, Lemon moved slowly through the lobby. Snickers, back on his normal leash, was in a much bigger hurry to get away from the torture chamber he'd been forced into. His attempts to sled dog the much bigger human had him moving in a zig zag pattern across the floor.

Weaving precariously through the lobby with a still blinded human attached to his lead, Snickers managed to weave his leash around someone's legs. Lemon reeled him in and scooped him up. "I'm so sorry." Her gaze slid up to a familiar face. "Ron."

The loud sniffing sound created by the powerful nose of a hound hit Lemon's ears at the same time the nose nudged her leg. She shifted Snickers in her arms and squatted down to pet Milo.

"Hi, Lemon." Ron's deep voice carried pleasant surprise.

Mei hadn't mentioned that her boss was coming down today. "Getting a picture taken with Milo?"

"Yes. It was my sister's idea. And when I mentioned it to Mei, she insisted we come down." He cocked his head. "Are you here helping?"

"No, actually, we got our picture taken. Snickers is staying with me now."

"Oh, Jillian's dog."

"Yeah."

The discomfort that always accompanied discussions of the recently deceased packed the space between them. Lemon opened her mouth to make whatever excuse to leave she could muster, when Ron spoke. "I suppose it's been a bit of a wild ride since you found the…foot."

So Ron officially knew now. That was unfortunate. "Technically Milo found the foot, not me." As soon as the words slipped out of her mouth, Lemon was swamped with regret.

Ron's eyes grew wide as his gaze shifted down to the dog lying in a heap at his feet. "Milo?"

"Um, yeah, sorry. I didn't really mean to tell you that."

After an excruciating beat, he returned his focus to Lemon. "I guess I shouldn't be surprised. He's got a hell of a nose."

The last thing Lemon intended was to drive a rift between a man and his dog. But Ron's little grin at the end of his statement gave Lemon some relief. Hopefully Ron wouldn't hold the creep factor against his pup.

Rearranging her entire walking schedule had been easier than the simple act of stepping through the large, glass doors of Noth, Inc. on Monday afternoon. She couldn't stroke Snickers' fur for comfort. Tucked away into a carrier slung over Lemon's shoulder, he was still and quiet, probably curious as to what the hell Lemon was thinking. It was a valid question.

"You got this," Mei whispered in her ear.

Mei's background in theater and her substantial experience with harmless deception, mostly of her own parents, probably bolstered her confidence in this crazy scheme. Lemon, on the other hand, sported a terrible case of stage fright and earned a solid C- in duplicity.

Having her dreams of abandoning the entire scheme dashed by text message, Lemon had followed Mei to the glass and steel high rise that housed the tech company. She'd been certain that her lame text telling Mike she was in the neighborhood with Snickers and wanted to stop by his office would be met with a polite rebuke. But instead of saying he was too busy or engaged in a meeting, Mike had invited her to come on up with the dog.

Now, as Lemon stepped over the Noth logo embedded in the marble floor on the twenty-sixth floor of the high rise nestled in the Financial District, she shivered. Mei walked confidently beside her, a crooked smile plastered on her face.

"Hi there," Mei said, her voice way too high-pitched. "We have an appointment to see Mike Ross."

That was an overstatement in Lemon's opinion. They were barging in where they didn't belong, searching for something they had no right to search for. But yeah, sure, they had an appointment.

The man behind the richly detailed front desk smiled at them. "Wonderful! May I tell him your names?" His eyes flashed to the dog carrier dangling from Lemon's shoulder.

Mei continued to speak for them both. "Please tell him that Lemon Lister is here with his mother's dog."

The mention of Mike's mother sent the previously still man into a fit of motion. His fingers flew across a tiny, white keyboard before punching wildly at a phone while jamming the receiver against his ear. "Mr. Ross. There is a woman here, actually two women, and one of them is…oh, I see. Yes, sir. Right away." He slammed the receiver down and peered up at Mei. "Please follow me." He jumped out of his seat and rounded the desk to lead the way.

Lemon took up the rear of the train as they hustled down a wide, carpeted hallway as if they were headed to a fire. When they reached a non-descript door, the receptionist wrapped on it rapid fire. A muffled response had him swinging the door open and ushering the visiting trio into a square office with a single, ordinary window providing scant light that hovered over a wooden desk.

Mike sat behind the desk, his face lit up as if he were greeting the Queen herself. He stood quickly, dismissed the receptionist, and held his hand out to Mei. "So nice to see you again!"

Mei pumped his hand before stepping aside to make way for Lemon and her luggage to approach Mike. He reached out his hand again, his eyes shining in a way they never had at Friday night's dinner. Lemon took it. His grip was firm but his soft palm contrasted to Lemon's leash-worn callouses.

"Please sit down," Mike said. He held his hand toward the chairs that sat opposite his desk.

Mei sat quickly. Lemon moved more purposefully, carefully shifting the carrier to her lap as she lowered herself into the chair.

Mike's gaze touched the carrier again. "How is he?"

"He's good. Can I let him out in here?" Lemon looked over her shoulder to ensure that the receptionist had closed the door, the fear of Snickers running rampant down the hallway flashing through her brain. But it stood completely closed.

"Yes. Please," Mike said.

Lemon sat the crate on the floor and ran the zipper around the opening, releasing Snickers from his temporary prison. He immediately scampered out, his soft fur rising up with static electricity, leaving him looking a bit like one of those dolls with the crazy hair that can be purchased at a gas station.

Mike pushed his chair away from his desk, pressing the wheels against the wall just below the window. He bent over, clapping his hands together. "Come here, Snickers."

Snickers looked back at Lemon, a question in his soft, brown eyes. "Go on," she encouraged.

The little dog trotted around the desk, but then slowed, approaching Mike with his neck stretched out, nose quivering. Mike held out one hand. Lemon repressed the urge to tell him not to do that, to leave his hands at his sides and wait for the dog to approach. But every time she tried to instruct someone on the proper way to greet a dog, it backfired on her. So she kept her mouth shut.

The room seemed to be filled with tension as all the humans watched the small ball of fluff approach Mike one tentative step at a time. Every breath seemed to be held in anticipation as Snickers reached out each paw tentatively and moved toward Mike. Finally, his nose touched Mike's palm and a collective sigh filled the room.

To Lemon's great surprise, Mike slid off his chair, planting the seat of his dark jeans on the carpet. Snickers lay down in front of him and accepted his gentle pets.

"I guess you guys are close," Lemon said.

Mike gazed up at her. "Not really. I'm not a dog person or anything, not like my mom. I guess…" Mike stood suddenly, clearing his throat. "Listen, we should talk about why you came."

"Why I came?" Lemon tipped her head to the side. "I just thought you'd like to see Snickers."

Mike cleared his throat again. "Is there something else?"

In the worst possible moment, a brown messenger bag snagged Lemon's gaze as it hung precariously off the back of Mike's desk chair. Lemon nearly choked. What could she possibly say? Yes. Actually, we came to find out what's in your bag. Probably not a good approach.

"I think Lemon is missing your mom, to be honest," Mei said. She took a step forward, drawing Mike's attention.

"Oh," Mike's eyes drifted between both women. "I thought…"

"What?" Lemon asked.

Mike frowned. "I thought maybe you wanted some money…you know, for Snickers upkeep. And that's fine if you do. I'm totally prepared to, ya know…"

Lemon shook her head so violently, a tear that unexpectedly leaked from her eye flew off her cheek. Her sudden emotion played perfectly into Mei's crazy plan, but she didn't really care. "No. No. Not all. To be honest." Lemon swallowed hard. "I love having Snickers. My parents took off to Costa Rica and left me in this big apartment. And as stupid as it sounds, I wasn't really ready to be alone yet. I mean I had roommates all through college, and then I was looking forward to living with my parents for at least, like, six months or something now that I'm not a terrorist teenager. I thought we could enjoy each other for a little while before I moved out on my own. Not that I could afford to move…" Lemon bit her lip to stop herself from continuing to ramble like an idiot.

"Mike, maybe Lemon could use a cup of tea or something," Mei suggested.

"Um, yeah, of course." Suddenly closer, Mike's voice dripped with concern and regret. "Come with me, we've got tea and coffee just down the hall."

Lemon resisted the urge to exchange a glance with Mei. This wasn't part of their plan. Mike was supposed to offer to go get something and leave them alone in the room.

"That's a great idea," Mei said. "I'll just wait here with Snickers."

Even as she stood and took Mike's offered arm, Lemon reeled from Mei's genius suggestion. Not only did it give Mei alone time with the bag, it kept Lemon from having a panic attack during the actual snooping. She simply wasn't cut out for espionage. Mei on the other hand should work for the CIA.

Keenly aware that the scheme hung on her ability to keep Mike engaged, Lemon racked her brain for suitable conversation as they drifted down the hall. Mike suddenly pivoted, turning into an open doorway. The bright lights and tile-covered floor left no room for mistaking this space as anything other than a break room.

Mike settled Lemon at a plastic chair with a swooping, curved back before heading to an electric kettle. He scooped the kettle off its base and filled it, still silent, giving Lemon more time to attempt to get her mind moving. By the time he settled the kettle back on its base, Lemon grasped onto a safe subject for discussion. "My mother says that she thinks the Legion will name a gallery for your mother. Is that true?"

Mike smiled fondly, and nodded. "Yes. News must travel fast. George Nichols just called me to tell me about it yesterday."

"Oh…George called you?"

"Yeah. He was the one who pushed it through. I mean, I don't think it was a hard sell or anything. He said the Board vote was unanimous. I told him I thought they should wait a little while to make it official though. I mean at least until we have…you know…some more information."

Bubbling emanated from the kettle as it reached a fever pitch. Mike jumped up as if he needed to rescue it from a predator, but once he turned the power off, his movements became slow and deliberate. He carefully chose a mug from a crowded shelf, pulling out several rejects before plucking a mug featuring a smiling Golden Retriever from the deep recesses of the shelf. He then scrubbed the mug with ferocity before giving it a long, languishing rinse. After a thorough drying and finally teabag insertion and meticulous pour, he presented the mug to Lemon and shifted into the seat opposite her.

Lemon bobbed the teabag in her cup and smiled at Mike. "Thank you so much."

"Listen, I didn't mean to upset you earlier. To be honest, I've always been suspicious of them. Ever since my parents' divorce it feels like most of the people in my mother's life are always after something from her. It's made me very cynical. But I can see that you genuinely care about Snickers. It was wrong of me to assume otherwise."

"I genuinely liked your mother." Lemon threw the truth out before she took a gingerly sip of tea. The smooth liquid slid down her throat and helped to break up the lump there. Her mother was right. Tea could fix almost anything.

Mike smiled. "I appreciate that."

They sat in silence for a few minutes, each independently tending to wounded souls while in the company of a fellow sufferer. The space between the sound of Lemon's sips and Mike's fingertips sliding slowly over the tabletop became so familiar that when it was punctured by the squeak of rubber soles on the linoleum floor, they both jumped.

"Hi Naomi," Mike said to the newcomer.

The woman smiled and greeted them both before swinging over to the refrigerator. Mike stood, clearing his throat loudly. Completely unsure of how much time had passed, but hoping it was enough, Lemon stood as well.

Mike discarded Lemon's teacup five times faster than he retrieved it, and in seconds flat he ushered her back down the hall to his office. He stopped in front of it, staring at the closed door.

"Something wrong?" Lemon asked, her voice ridiculously loud. Her hopes that it penetrated the wood and reached Mei's ears didn't make it any less out of place in the quiet office.

"Oh, I didn't close the door when we left."

"Yeah, Mei probably had to. You know, to keep Snickers from following me."

Mike chuckled. "Sure, right. I forgot there was a dog in my office." He pushed open the door.

Mike didn't step aside to let Lemon enter first this time, so she had to crane her neck to see around his shoulders. Mei stood behind Mike's desk, her phone held in front of her like a camera, her back to the door.

Lemon's heart leapt into her throat as Mike's voice echoed through the room. "What are you doing?"

Snickers barked. Mei spun around, a huge smile on her face. "Getting a picture. The view is amazing from this high up."

"Oh, sure. Well, there's a better view on the roof if you want to go up there and check it out." Mike shoved his hands in the front pocket of his jeans.

"Maybe another time," Lemon said. "I have more dogs to walk today."

"Right. Yeah." Mike stepped aside, allowing Mei and Snickers to pass by him on their way to Lemon and the room's exit. "Well, thanks for stopping by. It was nice to see you and Snickers."

Lemon and Mei smiled, waved, and said some parting things Lemon was barely conscious of before hightailing it down the hallway and back to the elevator. When the thick, metal doors slid shut and they descended through the building, Lemon finally took a breath.

"Damn, that was some quick thinking, Lister." Mei held up her phone. "And whatever you did to keep him out so long, it worked. I got a picture of every single page."

"I feel like a criminal," Lemon mumbled.

"You always say that. And what do I always tell you?"

"That I'm not technically the criminal, just an accomplice"

Mei grinned at her. "Though to be fair, I don't break the law on the regular."

That was true. Mei was no felon. She just thought rules were meant to be bent a bit, whereas Lemon saw them as immovable. "I was totally scared."

Mei patted her back. "You did great." Then she bent over and scratched Snickers' fluffy head. "And so did you sweetheart. Now we just need to find out what the hell all those papers say."

Lemon glanced at Mei and bit her lip. "What if it's not important to the murder."

Mei shrugged. "Then it's not. No harm no foul. But what if it is? What if it's the key?"

That's exactly what Lemon was really afraid of.

CHAPTER ELEVEN

It might have been the most exciting Monday night at Lemon's house in months. Instead of eating leftovers in front of her computer while sending invoices to customers and paying bills, Lemon, Mei, and Jade munched on nachos fresh out of the oven and passed around the printed images from Mei's phone.

"So it's clearly a will," Jade said. "And the date indicates that Jillian changed it recently."

Mei said, "One day shy of a month before her death to be exact."

Lemon's stomach quivered. The more they dug into this the more it felt like the plot of a true crime documentary. "Is there a way to find out what the changes are?"

Jade shook her head. "This isn't a mark-up version. There's no way to know for sure. This could even be the first will she ever wrote, though I doubt it."

"I wonder if there's a way to find out, like by contacting the lawyer that's listed here," Lemon said.

"One thing at a time," Jade said. "We need to figure out what's in this one first."

Mei stuck up one finger. "And we can't exactly call the lawyer and say we saw Jillian's will because I riffled through her son's bag and took pictures of it."

Lemon scooped Snickers up in her lap and leaned back. "Reading this legalese is making my eyes water. I'll let you two tell me what you find."

"Okay, Communications major, way to be a quitter," Mei said.

"The things I studied were interesting." Lemon gave Snickers' ear a good scratch. "Way more interesting than forensic science or art history. So, yeah, I'll leave the hard stuff up to you two."

Jade flashed Lemon a sweet smile before returning her attention to the papers. Lemon spent her time giving Snickers good boy scritches and watching as Jade's brow wrinkled in concentration.

"Okay, this is super interesting," Mei said. "Mike gets all of Jillian's money."

"That's not surprising," Lemon said. "She was divorced and he's her only child."

"Yeah, but here's the thing," Mei said. "She only left him her money, not the stock she owned in Noth, Inc."

"So, what does that mean?" Lemon asked.

"It means he doesn't gain controlling interest," Jade said. "Which I'm sure he expected to get when she died."

"I need more," Lemon said.

Mei dropped the paper on the table and pinned her gaze on Lemon. "It's really interesting, actually. See. Jillian owned forty-one percent of the company. Mike inherited ten percent from his grandfather. If Mike inherited Jillian's shares, he'd have control of the company. But she didn't leave her shares to him."

"Who did she leave them to?"

"Various charities," Jade said. "Six different ones. They will most likely sell the shares for the cash."

"Okay, wait." Lemon rubbed her forehead. "So if Mike owns ten percent and Jillian owned forty-one percent. Who owned the other forty-nine percent?"

Jade and Mei exchanged a glance and shrugged. "The will doesn't say," Mei said.

"If I had to guess," Jade said, "I would say probably a few cousins and some other investors, maybe relatives of original investors or people they sold them to."

"Okay, so she kind of screwed Mike out of having controlling interest in the company. What does that really mean?"

"It means, "Mei said, "he can't ever take control, appoint himself the CEO or president of the board, or whatever else he wants."

"He doesn't strike me as a power grabber. Maybe that isn't as important to him as you are assuming it is," Lemon said. She couldn't think that Mike was capable of matricide, not after seeing him with Snickers. Not after their exchange in the break room. Not over something as petty as shares to a company.

"Have you met his wife?" Mei raised her eyebrow. "Whatever you may think of Mike, you must see that he's not in control in that household. He does what Tina wants him to do, and Tina sure as shit is a power grabber."

"I guess, but I still don't think he'd kill his mom over this," Lemon said. "Besides, if you're going to kill someone for what's in their will, don't you want the body to be found so you can collect? I mean, that's usually a thing with the insurance scams and stuff on the true crime podcasts."

"Hence the feet," Jade said. "Get rid of the body so we can't figure out why or how she died or have any evidence of who killed her. But leave the feet somewhere they would be found and then she can be pronounced dead."

Lemon bit the edge of her lip. "Buried where only a hound dog could find it?"

Mei slid over Lemon's logic. "There's more." Her nose once again buried in one of the papers, she spoke while her eyes continued to travel from left to right. "The house goes to Nancy."

"Nancy?" A thick glob of confusion stuck in Lemon's throat. "The house?"

"Yep," Mei said. "And everything in it." She looked up, her eyes wide. "It's worth millions. No doubt about it."

"And that, my friends," Jade said. "Gives us a new suspect."

Without the other dogs along, and with little resistance from Lemon, Milo followed his nose. Lemon's favorite pair of sneakers and shorts made it easier to follow along, gripping the bungie-style leash with one hand and pushing aside errant branches with the other.

The only will Lemon asserted on the big-eared sniffing machine was to start their journey at the approximate location of the foot find. From there, she let the hound take over. He pulled her through the Eucalyptus grove, past the picnic tables, and across the parking lot to the area around the Legion of Honor.

Milo's nose practically made love to the nearly century-old stone. He lingered around the building's cornerstone for a moment. But instead of providing some great clue, it served a different purpose, which became apparent when he lifted his leg and unloaded on it.

After his brief break, Milo caught the scent again, leading Lemon along the line of the building until they reached the courtyard. It opened up in front of Lemon, the stone arch providing a regal entrance. Milo raced toward the masterpiece sitting in the center of the courtyard.

One of a couple dozen casts of Rodin's "The Thinker", the piece stood as a reminder that another nearly one hundred original Rodin sculptures lived inside the regal building. Milo's concern, however, remained with the scents of the living rather than the legacies of the dead. He pivoted, plowing through a small gathering of tourists.

Lemon attempted to apologize as people shuffled to move out of Milo's way. But keeping up with short legs proved more difficult for her the closer he got to the building's entrance. Leaving every stereotype about the plodding nature of Bassett Hounds in his figurative dust, he plowed forward on a mission only he and his olfactory receptors were aware of.

When he waltzed up to the front door, Lemon finally pulled back on the leash, coaxing him to the side to prevent the opening door from clocking him in his huge noggin. She felt like an idiot. Milo wasn't on any feet-finding mission. He was simply looking for his dad, Ron, who was inside working.

Lemon crouched down beside the pooch, who whined in protest of not getting what he wanted. Concentrated on providing the most soothing chest rub she could muster, Lemon failed to pay attention to the the people bursting out of the door until one nearly ran into her and the miserable pup in her arms.

Lemon craned her head up to see who had stopped abruptly in front of them. Tall, and as always, muscular, George Nichols also looked imposing.

"Lemon?"

"Hi, George."

"What are you doing here?" His tone was harsher than she was accustomed to. Lemon expected the usual gentle giant routine from George. The large man squeezing his sweet little pup, Klee, after he returned home was a far cry from the man looming over her now.

Lemon stood. While it closed the distance, it didn't prevent her from still having to crane her neck to meet his gaze. "I was just walking Milo and, apparently he wanted to visit his dad, Ron. He works inside." Of course, George as a board member most likely knew that, and she mentally slapped her hand to her forehead over the idiotic statement.

"Why would you even have a dog in this area? The grass is over there." Keeping his steely gaze pinned on Lemon, he swung his arm as far behind him as humanly possible and stuck his finger toward the golf course beyond the foot-finding forest.

A knot stuck in the pit of Lemon's stomach. She'd never made a client angry like this. "I was letting him sniff. You know, to see if he could find out what happened to Jillian."

She hoped that telling George her motives would help her cause. She expected his demeanor to change, and it did. But the transformation did not fit the playbook.

"What? Why the hell would you do that?" Flames of color licked up his neck, turning his face bright red.

"What?" Confusion and a touch of fear swamped Lemon. "I mean. I just want to know what happened to her."

George took a step, bringing his face so close to Lemon's she instinctively jerked back. His voice, softer now, was far more menacing. "Didn't it occur to you how dangerous that might be? Leave that to the police." He straightened up suddenly, his eyes scanning the space around them. "Just find another place to walk the dogs, okay?"

"Yeah, okay. I will. Sorry."

He grumbled and stared out at Rodin's Thinker perched in the courtyard. "I will be leaving a folder with Klee's updated vaccination paperwork and pet insurance information by the door. Pick that up when you get him today. I won't be there."

"Sure. No problem."

Without glancing her way again, George marched through the courtyard toward the parking lot, his back straight, jaw set in a straight line. He shoved his way through clumps of observers, many with looks of concern or curiosity painting their faces. Lemon's own face probably reflected something very different.

Clutching Klee to her chest, Lemon knocked on the door one last time. Just like it had a couple hours earlier, it remained unanswered. As she retrieved the key, her intense anxiety eased.

Seeing George again after witnessing his flared temper earlier that day was at the very bottom of Lemon's to-do list. While she didn't expected him to be home when she picked Klee and his paperwork up, the entire time she walked Klee and the other evening crew pups, she agonized over what would happen at their meeting when she dropped Klee off.

She now faced an empty condo once again. After closing the door and relieving Klee of his harness and leash, Lemon crept cautiously into the living room. The blanket that hung off the back of couch still featured a large wrinkle. The magazine on the coffee table still lay with its spine up and it open pages down. Klee's squeaky toy still sat directly in the path to the kitchen.

Lemon fed Klee his dinner and refreshed his water dish. She left a pink sticky note stuck to the refrigerator to indicate what she'd done. Then she gave Klee a quick kiss and scurried out as if the empty condo might eat her alive.

With only Tilly to drop off, Lemon carefully drove the three blocks to Nancy's house and hopped out of the van as if it had bit her. She scooped Tilly out of the back and practically ran toward Nancy's door.

As she rang the bell, Lemon's mind teased her with the vision of another empty house, another client she couldn't lay eyes on. All part of the trauma of Jillian's death she knew, but no less real.

Thankfully, Nancy threw the door open. Her bright smile and open arms as she reached for Tilly further slowed Lemon's runaway train heartbeat. She assessed Nancy's demeanor as she followed the woman into her living room. Nothing out of the ordinary here. Lemon let out a long breath.

"Are all the dogs dropped off? Can I get you a cup of tea before you head home?"

"You know, that would be great." Lemon dropped into the recliner and leaned back.

Thinking she would have more time to process, Lemon shot up in surprise when Nancy rapidly returned with a teacup. "I was just making some when you arrived," she explained.

Lemon thanked her and cradled the mug to her chest. "It's been a long day."

Nancy sat down across from her, and Tilly hopped into her lap. "Oh no. What happened, sweetheart?"

Lemon was happy to unload to the one person who best understood her pain over Jillian. It didn't hurt that she held a strong belief that Nancy herself was not involved in the death. Not that Nancy knew Lemon's friends had her on their suspect list.

"I had a strange interaction with George Nichols today."

Nancy's penciled-in eyebrows raised. "Oh yeah? Strange how?"

"He was very…gruff with me. Like angry. He's always been very nice in the past."

"Hmm. He was probably just having a bad day. You haven't known him that long. Like everyone, he isn't always happy-go-lucky."

"Yeah, I get that. But it was really out of the ordinary."

Nancy shrugged.

"Also, he wasn't there when I picked up or dropped off Klee. I had to feed Klee his dinner."

"Maybe he was busy."

Lemon leaned forward, overwhelmed. "I ran into him at the museum."

Nancy leaned forward as well, her elbows on her knees. Tilly huddled into the space between her thighs and her chest. "I had dinner with him last night. He mentioned he was headed to the museum today. There's nothing strange here, Lemon."

Wholly unaware of the expression on her own face, Lemon scanned Nancy head to toe not finding anything useful in her demeanor. "But, don't you think it's a little strange? Taken altogether, I mean."

Nancy scooped Tilly up, pressing her to her chest and stood. "I think you are suffering from PTSD, my dear. Jillian's death has affected you deeply, understandably. And now you are terrified that all of your clients are in danger." Nancy pulled the tea from Lemon's hand and set in on an end table. She cupped her hand around Lemon's upper arm and tugged. Taking the hint, Lemon heaved herself out of the chair. "I think you should go home and get some sleep, sweetheart. I bet you haven't been sleeping well, have you?"

"Not really."

Nancy patted her arm. "Take some melatonin and get a good night's sleep, dear. Everything will be fine in the morning."

While her food circled lazily in the microwave, she called George. No answer. Straight to voicemail. As soon as she was done eating, she tried again. Same result.

Lemon dropped the last bits of the leftovers she just couldn't manage to swallow down and stared at Snickers' dog bowl. It was empty, of course, she'd fed him as soon as she came home from Nancy's. She also checked her emails, updated her schedule, and eaten dinner.

Lemon glanced at the clock. It was nearly nine. If George wasn't home, that meant Klee was still alone. Lemon took a deep breath and made a decision: dog welfare definitely beat potential embarrassment.

She grabbed her keys and drove to George's house. She hopped out and sprinted to the door. For the third time that day, there was no answer when she knocked.

Once again, Lemon let herself in. Klee greeted her with enthusiasm. He jumped up and pressed his paws against her shins. His whine was accompanied by the smell of his urine.

Lemon examined the puddle at her feet. Klee hadn't been out since she'd dropped him off. His dad hadn't been home. Lemon watched enough true crime to know what that meant. In all the true crime episodes, one thing stood out. People never left the dog unattended to unless they were kidnapped or dead.

She scooped Klee up and left the house.

CHAPTER TWELVE

Lemon's knee bounced up and down erratically. Klee didn't verbally protest, but he did shift his chin so it rested on her still knee. The dramatic sigh that accompanied the move registered his annoyance.

Lemon's back molded into the unforgiving metal chair, seriously unhappy about the torture it had been enduring for the last forty minutes. A police officer arrived in the lobby and called for a Mel Smith before leading the middle-aged man through a secure door.

Not unlike waiting in an emergency room, this too held the pain of boredom and the anxiety of what was to come. So, when Mei breezed through the double doors Lemon nearly crumpled in relief.

Mei's strong, secure hug elicited a squeak of protest from Klee. "Sorry, baby." Mei patted his silky grey head, proving once again how far she'd come in overcoming her phobia. Klee licked her fingers. Mei dropped into the seat beside Lemon, her expression reflecting the discovery of exactly how hard and unforgiving the thing was.

"You talk to anyone yet?"

"No. Apparently, I'm on a long list." Lemon nodded toward the desk, which was intermittently staffed by a cranky-looking older woman and a stern-faced young man.

"So, have you tried calling George?"

"Of course I have."

Mei shimmied Lemon's phone out her pocket and scrolled through it. "Hmm. Let me try again." She hit a button and stuck the phone to her ear. Ninety seconds later she held the phone back out to Lemon. "Straight to voicemail."

Lemon took the phone and shoved it back into her pocket. "Told you."

Mei sighed. "How long are we going to have to sit here?"

"You have literally been here for two minutes."

"Did you text Jade?"

"No." After texting Mei she'd been struck with insecurity. What if she was over-reacting? The last thing she wanted was to look like a fool in front of Jade as George came waltzing into the police station demanding his dog back.

"Ugh. I don't understand you. Well, good thing I texted her. She should be here any minute. She lives close."

Lemon would have berated Mei, but she had no idea what to say. And even if she was able to come up with something, she would have stopped short anyway as Jade stormed through the doors looking like she'd just come in from a winter blizzard rather than a San Francisco September.

Jade flew over to Lemon and Mei. "George is missing?"

"I mean, I can't find him," Lemon said. "So I think so."

"How long have you been sitting here?"

Lemon glanced at the big black and white analog clock on the far wall, its round face transporting her out of the modern tech city and back in time. "About forty-five minutes, I guess."

"Hang on," Jade said. She spun on her heel and marched over to the desk. Her demeanor instantly changed as she approached the officer. Her head cocked, her arms swooped out and her tone grew higher and lighter.

Mei and Lemon couldn't hear exactly what she said to the woman, but whatever it was earned a small smile and a nod followed by the woman picking up the phone receiver.

A few minutes later, Jade greeted a man emerging out of the interior doors in full SFPD uniform. They spoke for a minute, both smiling, faces soft. Then Jade gestured for Mei and Lemon to follow her.

Lemon tucked Klee into her elbow and rose. She followed Mei toward Jade, her steps slow and hestitant. Doubt attempted to drag her back to her apartment where there would be no potential false alarms, no one pulling strings to hear her story—which could very well be nothing at all.

On the edge of flight or fight—with flight being the most definite choice—Lemon was distracted by Klee's wet tongue darting out to lick her thumb. This was why she was here, causing so much trouble. George Nichols would never abandon his dog.

With a new boost of confidence, Lemon caught up to the clump of people ahead of her in the long, narrow, hallway. Each footstep echoed in the concrete hall like the ominous tones of catacombs leading to a dark and mysterious place.

Eventually they were seated in a small, windowless room, crammed around an oval table. The officer kept a large personal space for himself, forcing Jade, Mei, Lemon, and Klee to press against one another in a way that was both comforting and stifling.

The officer turned his bright blue eyes to Lemon. "I'm Bart Mcgee. I'll be taking your report today. Who are you?"

"Lemon Lister."

The man wrote down her name then peered back up her wordlessly. Lemon elaborated, "I'm the dog walker."

"Okay. And you?" He turned to Mei.

"Mei Lu. The dog walker's best friend."

He took a note before smiling at Jade. "And hi, Jade. How did you get involved in this?"

"These are my friends, and when they said they were down at the police station, I came right over to help out. I'm sure you'd do the same."

"Absolutely, I would. Who are we reporting missing?"

Lemon gave him George's name and address, after which he asked, "And how do you know he's missing?"

"He wasn't home when I went to pick up his dog this afternoon, or when I dropped him off. Then I tried calling all evening, and when he didn't answer I went to pick up Klee. But he still wasn't there and the house was in the exact same state as when I'd been there the first time." The story came out as one long string of words that once expelled, created a comfortable feeling of relief in her gut.

"When was the last time you saw Mr. Nichols?" Bart asked.

"Around noon."

Bart glared at her. "Noon when? Yesterday?"

"No. Today."

Bart's pen stopped moving. "Today? Like nine hours ago?"

Lemon nodded.

Bart dropped his pen. "Forgive me Ms. Lister, but what evidence do you have that he's not just in a meeting, or on a date, or out drinking with his buddies with a dead phone?"

Lemon lifted Klee up like he was Simba in the Lion King. "Because he left his dog. This man *loved* his dog."

"I get that. I really do." Bart's eyes grew soft as he gazed as Klee. "But you can leave a dog overnight."

Lemon tucked Klee back in her lap. "He would have called me if he was going to do that. In fact, last month he was going to be home late and he had me pick Klee up and keep him overnight."

Bart held up his hand. "Listen, I hear you. I do. But I can't call out the cavalry for a man for who's been gone as long as the average tech company work day. You understand, right?"

All of Lemon's insecurities rushed in, leaving her unable to speak. Fortunately, neither Jade nor Mei suffered from the same issue. They both spoke at the same time, creating cacophonous confusion. When they both stopped, Mei gestured to Jade, keeping her lips firmly closed.

"Bart, what would you say if I told you George was the vice president of the board of directors at the Legion?" Jade asked.

Bart's spine straightened, making him visibly taller. "Oh."

Mei leaned over the table. "Yeah. Oh."

Bart stood quickly, his chair screeching across the concrete floor. "I'll be right back."

As the door slammed shut behind the fleeing officer, Klee barked, registering his protest with the entire situation.

"Guess we should have led with that," Lemon said.

Jade chuckled. "You know what he's doing right now? Calling Detective Zahn. Guaranteed."

"Good," Mei said.

"But what if George *does* show up?" Lemon asked.

Jade met her gaze. "I seriously doubt he will. But if so, fine, whatever. It's not like you're going to get charged for being extra cautious, Lemon. And I mean, given that he's connected to a recently murdered person, it's not unreasonable."

"As evidenced by Officer Bart's reaction." Mei pointed at the closed door.

After a few minutes of waiting, Klee began to whine softly. "I think he has to pee."

"That's inconvenient," Jade said.

Lemon stroked Klee's ears. "Dogs are inconvenient. But they're also perfect."

Jade smiled. "You picked the right career."

"Technically it was thrust upon me, but yeah."

"She's right, though," Mei said. "I watch way too much true crime. And if they leave the dog behind, they're definitely dead."

Lemon covered Klee's ears. "I didn't say anything about him being…dead."

Mei shrugged. "What are the chances that he's tied up in a warehouse somewhere alive and waiting to be rescued? They aren't good, let me tell you."

Lemon slumped. A prickling sensation clawed at her eyes. She didn't think she could handle another death. She was still struggling with Jillian's likely murder. Not George, too.

Before Lemon could fall any further into the pit, Bart returned. He did not, however, sit back down at the table. He remained standing, his expression serious and tense. "Ms. Lister, I'm going to send you home tonight, but you can expect to hear from Detective Zahn in the morning."

"I freaking knew it," Jade said.

"You sound tired."

"Well, it is Wednesday." Lemon secured her ear pods and shoved the phone in her pocket, glad she wasn't on FaceTime so her mother couldn't see exactly how much she looked like she'd been run over twice by a Mack truck.

"Oh, and you were at the police station until late last night. That would definitely cause sleepiness."

Lemon sighed. "How did you know?"

"Guess."

Mei's mother had an unhealthy Facebook messenger relationship with Lemon's mom. It had caused more than a few problems in the past couple of years. "So, did she tell you why I was at the police station last night?"

"Sounds like you have another missing client."

Lemon sighed and slumped against the concrete wall. "I do." As if aware that his papa was the subject of conversation, Klee broke away from the romping pups in the center of the dog park and ran full tilt toward Lemon. She gave him a reassuring scratch beneath the chin and sent him back into the fray. "Did she tell you it was George Nichols?"

"Oh yeah. I mean, two missing board members." Her mother whistled. "Something is afoot at the Legion of Honor."

"You think?"

"What? You don't think it has something to do with the museum?"

"I mean, I guess that seems logical, but why would someone be kidnapping or killing people or whatever over art?"

"Oh sweetie, it's never about art. It's always about money."

There was more than one path in this mystery that led to cash. But Lemon wasn't up for explaining the murky clues they'd found so far. The jumbled mess of lines crisscrossing an imaginary bulletin board in her mind was beyond a simple phone conversation that spanned across continents.

"Well to make matters worse, Snickers and Klee don't get along."

"Oh, no!"

"Yeah, I've had them together in a pack with no problem. But for some reason when they had to share my bed last night, all hell broke loose. There was a massive fight over who got be on the bed and where. I finally managed to get them to agree on a sleeping arrangement at about two am. It sucked. But, anyway, tell me what's happening there. What's dad up to?"

Her mother launched into a story about her father, Madge, and Llamas. Lemon relaxed, lost in the story, and safe in her little dog park haven, when a newcomer opened the gate, creating a loud squeak that penetrated her ear buds. Lemon turned toward the entrance, as always interested in who came in and what breed of dog they brought with them.

But there was no dog with this newcomer. And he wasn't a stranger. Detective Zahn, dressed in a button-up shirt and grey slacks strode through the gate and was instantly swamped with enthusiastic canines.

He managed to give them each a paternal pat as he made his way across the Astroturf to Lemon's spot along the wall. He stopped a little way from her and shoved his hands in his pockets. "Good morning, Ms. Lister."

"Mom. I gotta go." Lemon hung up. "Lemon, please. Hi Detective. What are you doing here?"

He leaned against the concrete, mirroring Lemon's posture. "Looking for you."

"How did you know I would be here?"

Detective Zahn gazed out at the open area. "When you have regular patterns of movements it's only a matter of time before someone finds you."

"Well, that's creepy. Thanks."

Zahn laughed, the deep, baritone bouncing around in his chest. "Yes. I suppose so. Sorry about that." He gazed at Lemon with his bright, blue eyes, the crinkled edges giving away a propensity not to wear sunglasses. "I came to talk to you about George Nichols. I heard you reported him missing last night."

"I did. But I guess I didn't wait long enough. The officer didn't seem too interested. I mean, I could have jumped the gun."

"But?" Zahn prompted.

Lemon pointed toward Klee, who ran in a circle following Hedwig the Bichon, his tongue dangling out of the side of his mouth. "He left the dog behind."

"You did the right thing."

"I'm not sure the officer I talked to last night agrees."

"He does now." Zahn's tone contained no alarm, but the words grabbed Lemon's full attention.

"Why's that?"

"We can't find him either. And his boat isn't at the marina."

"His boat?"

"He has a small fishing vessel. We can't locate it. The Coast Guard is looking now."

"So, you think he took off in his boat?"

Zahn shrugged. "It's one possibility. What can you tell me about his daily routine?"

"Well, I take Klee out with my morning crew every day." Lemon slid her hand out toward the dogs as if she were the Vanna White of canines. "George is always home when I go to get him. He tends to have morning phone calls, I guess. I don't really know what it's about, just that he prefers to have Klee out of his hair. Then Klee comes back tired and George can get the rest of his work done."

"If you take Klee out in the morning, why were you there last night?"

"I offer evening walks to all my clients one day a week. The night I offer it changes. Usually, if one client requests a night—and it's often

Friday night—then I tell everyone else I will be doing a Friday night walk. George always takes me up on it, no matter what night it is. So, this week, I had a rare request for a Tuesday night from Betsy Cole. She has a sweet little pittie mix with a ton of energy and she was going out with a friend, and well, I told the rest of my clients I would be doing an evening walk and I did end up with four dogs. Betsy's dog, Kibble, Tilly, Milo, and Klee."

Zahn pulled a tiny paper notepad out of his pocket and flipped through it. "But George wasn't there during pick up or drop off?"

"No."

"And you said he was acting strange when you saw him that afternoon?"

"Yes."

"And did he say anything about your plans to walk his dog when you saw him?"

"Yes. He did mention it."

"And he remembered?"

Lemon fiddled with the edge of her backpack. "Yeah. He did. But he was…not mean as much as…just different toward me, and I wondered if I'd done something to make him angry. I guess it was obvious that there was something on his mind, something dark."

"Something dark? Like what?"

Lemon met Zahn's gaze. There was no confidence in her words, but she chose to say them anyway. "Like he was very upset about something and it was following him around. You know, like the cloud that hangs over Eeyore's head everywhere he goes?"

Zahn chuckled. "You paint quite the picture, Ms. Lister." He pushed off the wall. "Thank you for your time."

"Detective Zahn?"

"Hmmm?"

"Do you think…you could keep me, you know, informed?"

"Well, I tell you what. George Nichols doesn't have a lot of family, just a brother who lives in Europe. And since you have his dog, I guess that makes you my main contact. I'll be in touch."

"Thank you."

As Zahn swung open the waist-high gate to exit the park a cold dread filled Lemon. Somehow, she doubted that any of this would end well.

CHAPTER THIRTEEN

Lemon pulled the van up to a spot three houses down from George's. She knew from experience a closer spot would be impossible to get, so she took advantage of a free one rather than needlessly circling the block and wasting precious dog play time.

.This entire errand was probably a waste of time, but since it fit into her regular routine anyway, it seemed harmless. What if George had magically appeared overnight? She could picture him opening the door and reaching out his muscular arms to retrieve Klee from Lemon before cuddling the little fluffball and talking baby talk into the puppy's pert ears.

Still warmed by the image, she pulled Klee out of the back of the van, switched on the air conditioner, and told the rest of the dogs she'd be right back. She tucked Klee under one arm and headed up the sidewalk to George's stately Victorian.

They were still two houses away when Lemon spotted the flapping yellow ribbon. She inched close enough to hear the snapping of the tape in the breeze and read the black letters emblazoned on one side. Police Line. Klee couldn't read, but somehow he must have known those words meant his world had just turned upside down because he barked wildly and struggled to escape.

Klee's sad baying summoned the attention of one of the people huddled on George's porch. She peeled away and Lemon was happy to see that it was Jade walking toward them.

Jade's expression reflected the mood her presence at George's house created in Lemon. An inevitable sense of sadness replaced the constant dread and settled in her chest. It was firmly entrenched by the time Jade met up with Lemon and Klee where the sidewalk met the path to the house.

"Lemon." She stood very close. Her being nearby must have comforted Klee because he stopped his mournful howling and busied himself with a full olfactory exploration of Jade. "I'm very sorry."

Lemon's stomach dropped into her toes. "Is he…is he…in there?" The horrifying idea that she'd been in the house with George's dead body and somehow missed it loomed like a monster over all other thoughts.

"In there?" Jade threw her thumb over her shoulder while slowly bringing the other hand up to Klee's chin. "No, sweetie. He's not in the house. They found his boat last night. It was floating free in the Bay and he was inside…you know…dead." Even as she uttered that last word, the one that changed Klee's entire world, he accepted her touch, leaning in to get a gentle scratch beneath the chin.

"Oh wow. I mean…is there any chance he…you know…?"

"No. It was definitely murder. It'll be on the morning news." Jade glanced at her watch. "Any minute now. We already shooed the reporters away." She sighed heavily. "But the looky-loos will be by soon. We should get inside." She placed one hand on Lemon's elbow.

"Wait." Lemon's knees locked. "Why are we going in there?"

"Just into the foyer. I have fingerprinting stuff set up, and I need to get your prints. I can do it now and it will be easier than having you go down to the police station to do it."

None of that made Lemon's knees unlock, but it did create a steady shaking. "Wait. What? Why? What did I do?"

"Nothing. You didn't do anything. We just expect to find your prints in the house since we know you were in there getting the dog. We need to know which prints are yours versus someone else's. It's okay, Lemon, I promise."

Lemon managed to force her feet to move forward, following Jade's subtle tugging at her arm. "Okay. But I have dogs."

"I know, and that's why this will be easier for you. I promise."

Lemon kept her hands busy, giving Klee reassuring pats until Jade pulled her into the familiar entryway of George's house and used what appeared to be a fancy tablet to take electronic fingerprints. The entire thing took no time at all, and once she'd stepped back out onto the porch, leaving Jade to continue her work inside, Lemon finally drew in a real breath.

She stared at Klee for a beat, wondering if she should ask the half-dozen people roaming around inside with plastic booties and rubber gloves if she could grab some of his stuff. But it only took a second to abandon that idea, decide she'd use the pet store gift cards she'd been given by a few of her clients to get him what he needed, and raced to the van, anxious to be away from the death that seemed to be following her.

"I feel like this margarita was born to go with this taco." Mei held up her hands, each featuring one of the named items, her words muffled by a mouthful of street taco.

"Fuck yes," Jade agreed, her mouth equally as full, making it sound more like, "uck sss."

"I might have put some carnitas in Klee and Snickers dishes," Lemon admitted. She glanced over at the dogs. They stood on opposite ends of the kitchen, both their faces fully immersed in ceramic bowls, tongues eagerly licking at the now empty surface.

Jade swallowed. "They deserve it, poor babies."

Lemon watched the dogs as they abandoned their bowls and headed to the water fountain Lemon retrieved from Snickers house. Despite her fears of a fight, they took turns politely, Klee allowing Snickers to go first. "I'm trying to make them happy."

A hand fell on her knee. Lemon placed her own hand on top of

Jade's and took the comfort offered.

"And that is one reason why we have to figure out who the killer is," Mei said.

"Okay." Jade removed her hand from Lemon's knee to slap it on the table. "I'll put my ass on the line. At this point, this is too important." She glanced at the dogs again, both settled into a proper begging position at the base of Lemon's chair. "We found unknown fingerprints, meaning they don't match George, Lemon, or the cleaning lady, Mary."

Mei leaned forward "But can you find out who they belong to?"

"Two days of running them through the database and nothing so far. Also, the apartment isn't the murder scene."

Lemon let out an audible breath. "Thank God."

"What, you don't like the idea of having roamed around the crime scene?" Mei teased.

Lemon glared at her briefly before turning back to Jade. "So, do they know where he was killed?"

"Only that it's not the house or the boat."

"You were on the boat?" Mei asked.

"No. My colleagues processed it. The bottom line is, neither is the crime scene. And we don't know where it is."

Lemon stood and began gathering up plates. "Does that mean the killer took his dead body onto the boat?"

Jade handed over her empty plate with a smile. "It would seem so."

"Okay," Mei grabbed a rag from the top of the kitchen faucet and brandished it at Lemon and Jade. "Correct me if I'm wrong, but wouldn't it be hard to get a freaking body into a boat in a marina in the middle of San Francisco?"

"It's been done before," Jade said. "Nighttime is the right time."

Mei dropped the rag on the counter. "Still seems far-fetched."

"Far-fetched or not, someone did it, and they had an ingenious way." Jade reached across the island and grabbed the rag, running it over her side of the counter. "A group of drunken partiers did see someone hauling a giant box onto the boat. They actually asked the person what it was and the person said it was fishing gear. Only no box was found on the boat."

With no rag to demonstrate her frustration, Mei slammed a hand on the counter. "Damn."

Jade threw the rag back to her. "Yeah. It's a hot mess."

After placing the dishes in the sink, Lemon turned toward Jade. "Are you going to get in trouble for telling us all this?

"Some of it has been released to the press, like that the body was found on the boat. And they interviewed the drunken partiers last night. So, it's okay. Aside from the fingerprints, I didn't really tell you anything the press doesn't know."

Mei was in full Lois Lane mode. "Okay, but where does that leave everything?"

"Back at Jillian's will," Jade said.

Lemon hit Jade with her stare. She was not happy that they were edging their way back toward Mike. "What? What does George's death have to do with Jillian's will?"

"Everything." Mei pulled a pile of folded paper copies of pictures out of her bag. She unfolded them to reveal the images of Jillian's will they'd illicitly obtained from Mike's bag.

Jade touched the corner of one page with her finger. "See this?" She pointed to one word among a multitude on the page. "This is the name of the trust company George owns. Right here." She jammed her finger at the papers. "Locktite Trust. It's in the will because Jillian left George's company in charge of her shares of Noth, Inc. You know, the shares Mike expected to inherit but didn't. They were left to charity and George's company was in charge of them. Meaning that George probably knew about the will."

"Meaning," Mei took over, "that George probably knew who had the motive to kill Jillian."

"Maybe he even figured out who did it," Jade said.

"Which is why he was killed," Mei said.

Lemon hopped off the barstool, startling both dogs. "We have to stop. Now."

"What?" Mei and Jade asked at the same time.

"We have to stop trying to figure this out. Can't you see? This is dangerous. If what you are saying is true, then George was killed because he knew too much. We might be next."

Jade placed a hand on Lemon's shoulder. "Don't you see, Lemon. This is exactly why we have to keep looking. What if we're the only ones who can figure it out? What if we're the only ones who can stop the killings? We can't stop now."

Mei dropped a hand on her hip. "Lemon. Overcome your fear. Think of them." She pointed at the dogs. "Who will fight for them?"

Despite an urge to roll her eyes at Mei's pretense that her interest was for the dogs, Lemon simply nodded. She *did* care about the dogs, so she couldn't argue with that, as much as she wanted to.

After a long week filled with stress, anxiety, and few dog puke and poop issues, Lemon was definitely not interested in answering the phone before she'd even finished her coffee on Saturday morning, especially for a number she didn't recognize.

But when she played back the voicemail her apathetic attitude completely changed. The woman didn't say why she was calling, only that her name was Helen McBride, she was Jillian Ross's attorney, and she wanted Lemon to call her back.

Sitting on the literal edge of her seat, Lemon waited while the phone rang. Her mind raced through the maze of possibilities as to why Jillian's lawyer could possibly call her.

"McBride."

"Ms. McBride. This is Lemon Lister. You called me?"

"Oh, Lemon, hello." The woman's voice lightened, as if they were old friends. "Yes. Thank you for calling me back. I know it's a little strange to receive a call like this on a Saturday morning. I really need to figure something out, and I'm hoping you can help me."

"I can try."

"Great. First, I need to apologize for not calling you sooner. Mike told me you were taking Snickers and I really should have contacted you. I'll send you an email with the link to change his ID chip and the info for his vet."

"Oh, okay, that would be great. Thanks." The idea that someone would pay an attorney what was no doubt an insanely high hourly rate to keep track of their dog's data was beyond Lemon's ability to grasp.

"Good. I'll do that soon. But there's something else, something pressing. You see, I did a lot of things for Jillian, sensitive things. One of the things she asked me to do was keep a letter for George Nichols. I was to deliver it to him whenever she told me to. I know this sounds a little strange. But I didn't question it. To be honest, I have clients that ask for things like this. I get paid what I do because I execute their wishes exactly. However, in this case, it all went a little wrong. Jillian went missing before she ever told me to give the letter to George. I gave it to him after she was declared dead. And now he's gone."

"What was in the letter?"

"I don't know. I never opened it. But with two dead people on our hands, one of whom was my client and one of whom I saw less than forty-eight hours before his death, I am cooperating fully with the police, obviously. I told them about the letter, but they didn't find it at George's house. And I'm sure I don't need to tell you this is a high-pressure situation. I was racking my brains last night, and I wondered if you've seen it."

Lemon gripped the fabric of the couch. "What? How would I have seen it?"

"I just thought maybe, since you've been to the house to get the dog. I heard you had the dog, George's dog, that is. The police told me. They said you'd been to the house."

"I mean, yes, I have been to the house. But I didn't see any letter."

"Damn. All right. Thanks. I appreciate it."

"Sure."

"Listen, Lemon. If you suddenly think of something, will you let me know?"

"Yeah. Sure."

"Okay. Thanks. Take Care."

"You too." As she hung up the phone ribbons of anxiety roamed up Lemon's spine. What, exactly, was she in the middle of?

CHAPTER FOURTEEN

Lemon thought choosing a favorite gay bar in the Castro was like picking a favorite child. Mei didn't have that problem. Neither did Jade. Unfortunately, they didn't agree. But since the entire purpose of tonight was to meet up with Hayley, they went to *her* favorite place.

The little hole-in-the-wall bar was high on kitsch and low on volume, allowing them to actually engage in conversation. Lemon managed to avoid any conversation about her shitty week or the weird-ass conversations with cops and lawyers she'd had. Instead, their discussions flowed around their work and their families, what mutual friends were up to, and even what they'd been eating for dinner.

The inevitable finally happened, however, when Hayley turned the topic to the book club. "We're halfway to the next meeting. How are you all progressing on the book?"

A deep silence fell over the table, until Jade piped up. "I'm on chapter five. Not as far as I'd like to be, but I'll have more time to read this next week."

"I read the prologue," Mei said. "So, you know, I at least cracked the spine."

Hayley laughed. "You always wait until the last minute, Mei. What about you Lemon?"

All eyes landed on her, and Lemon squirmed. "I haven't actually started it yet."

Hayley touched Lemon's hand with a brief, gentle nudge. "I guess you've been kind of busy."

"It's been a long week, yeah."

"I'm sorry." Hayley said, "It must be hard on you. Not one, but two dead clients?"

"Wait." Mei jumped in her seat. "Wait. How did you know that?"

"Know what?" Hayley sat up straight, her eyes wide. "That George Nichols is dead? Everyone knows that. It's all over the news."

"No. I mean, how did you know he was one of Lemon's clients?" Mei asked.

"Oh," Hayley flailed her arms, nearly knocking Jade's martini glass off the end of the table. "You must have told me at some point, Lemon."

They all knew about Lemon's memory. Everyone in book club did. Lemon could recite a passage by heart that she read only once. She didn't show it off, but it was the kind of thing that was hard to hide in certain situations. Hayley knew, and that knowledge combined with what she said registered on her face.

Lemon decided to throw her a line. "Maybe I did."

Even as Mei's eyes narrowed, Hayley rescued herself. "Okay. The truth is..." She leaned back and folded her arms. "Nancy told me."

"Nancy, Jillian's best friend, Nancy?" Mei asked.

"Yes." Hayley's short response left little room for understanding.

"How do you know Nancy?" Jade asked, her voice in law enforcement mode.

Hayley rocked from side to side as if the chair she sat on for the last hour suddenly became unbearably uncomfortable. "I told you I worked for Jillian for a while. They're best friends. I used to see her from time to time, that's all."

"And you kept in touch with her?" Mei asked.

"Enough." Hayley stood so fast her chair scraped the floor with a loud squeak. "Oh man, I'm getting serious fuck me eyes from a woman at the bar. I gotta go check this out." She moved around the table and glanced back to her companions for a brief moment. "Don't wait up."

Then, with a wink, she was gone.

Mei clapped her hands. "Well, that was an abrupt exit."

"Because you guys were practically interrogating her," Lemon said.

Mei shrugged. "She's obviously hiding something. If she doesn't want to get questioned, she needs to learn to perfect her poker face. This is the second time she's gotten all squirrelly on us. It makes me think she knows something about both murders."

"What could she possibly know?" Lemon asked. "She's an accountant, not a CIA operative."

"You're downplaying what accountants know," Jade said. "Especially accountants who work for rich people."

"Why do I continually feel like I'm trapped in an episode of *Dateline*?" Lemon said.

Jade spread a hand over her knee under the table. "Because you kind of are."

Lemon sighed. "Yeah. And I wish it was over."

"Speaking of which," Mei said, "we need to talk about this connection between Nancy and Hayley."

"It's probably exactly what she said it was. They know each other through Jillian and they kept in touch," Lemon said.

Mei patted Lemon's cheek. "It's adorable how much you trust people."

Lemon yanked her chin out of Mei's reach. "It's disgusting how cynical you are."

Mei grinned. "We're yin and yang, baby."

"Okay," Jade said. "I'm going to step in here and say I agree with Mei. I've known Hayley for a year and a half, and I've never seen her act so weird. Two people are dead and we're talking in circles. What did she know about Jillian's finances that was so mysterious, and why is her relationship with Nancy such a hush-hush thing? I just…Something is up." Jade glanced at the bar where Hayley was deep in conversation with a hot brunette with tight curls and legs for days.

Lemon ran through every bit of information gathered so far, the pieces all crooked and sitting in jumbled piles. Nothing fit together. But to make matters worse, Lemon was certain nothing could make it all form a complete picture without the still missing pieces.

As the door swung open, Tilly bolted out, jumped up, her claws sharp against Lemon's cotton leggings. Lemon scooped her up before she could wander out onto the sidewalk.

"This is such a nice surprise," Nancy said. She ushered Lemon in and sat her down in the recliner while she fussed over getting her a cup of tea. "I put the pot on as soon as I got your text message."

"That's sweet, thank you." Lemon accepted Tilly as a lap blanket and tracked Nancy's movements from the living room to the kitchen and back. "I'm sorry to intrude on such short notice."

"Don't be silly. Tilly and I were just watching our Sunday morning shows, doing nothing special. Having a guest is much more entertaining." Carefully balancing two matching mugs in her hands, she passed one to Lemon.

Lemon took the mug and cupped it in both hands. She waited until Nancy was seated on the couch across from her before she dove into her inquiries. "I was hoping you could answer some questions for me about Jillian."

Nancy smiled. "I can sure try, sweetheart."

"Well," Lemon glanced down at her cup, seeking courage in its liquidy depths. "I was wondering about her will."

"Oh." An exaggerated nod accompanied her long, drawn-out syllable. "Sure. You're wondering if Snickers is in it?"

"Well, no. I actually talked to the lawyer and she said he wasn't. I mean, she didn't tell me anything else about the will, just that Snickers isn't in it."

"But he is," Nancy said.

"He is?"

"Yes. He's listed as part of the things that go with the house."

"I see." Lemon ran her fingers through Tilly's fur.

"And Jillian left me the house."

"She did?" Lemon feigned surprise.

"Ummm hmmm."

"I'm surprised. I mean, I guess I thought she'd leave it to Mike."

"Nope. Me." Nancy sipped her tea.

"So, did you want Snickers then? Since I guess he would actually go to you. "

"Oh, heavens no! Tilly needs to be an only child, don't you baby?" She made kissy noises at Tilly. The little dog leapt off Lemon's lap and sprinted across the room to greet her mama. "I appreciate that you took Snickers in. I really do." She smiled at Lemon. "If I find any more of his things, I'll let you know. Good heavens, there is so much!"

"Oh?"

"Yes." Nancy sighed. "The police released the house to me. And don't get me wrong, I'm not in any hurry to clear away Jillian's stuff. But I do need to go through her papers. And it's giving me a migraine."

"You know, I was actually wondering about the paperwork as well."

"Oh of course, you probably want Snickers records." Nancy wiped her brow. "I'll get to them, I promise. It's just…" A heaviness drifted off Nancy, one Lemon hadn't recognized before, but she realized now had always been there, since they first realized Jillian might be gone.

"No. That's not it actually. I mean, I do need all of his things. But I was wondering if Jillian had anything that mentioned George Nichols. Like paperwork or something?"

"You mean because he held the trust for her? Probably. I don't know." Nancy stood, suddenly and abruptly, and left living room. Tilly trotted along behind her.

When she returned, she presented an overflowing folder to Lemon. Lemon needed both hands to take the thick, heavy object. The binding of the folder strained around the massive quantity of paper. "This is everything I found in her desk drawer. There's a filing cabinet, too, but I haven't even touched that yet. She always told me all the important stuff was in the top drawer. So that's where this is from. Feel free to sort through it." She dropped down heavily on the couch. "In fact, I'd appreciate it if you did."

Lemon thanked Nancy and, with a few kind words, left. After stopping for the largest possible latte, she took herself, her drink, and the overflowing folder to her kitchen island. She pulled each piece of paper out, read through it and placed them into neat piles identified by purpose with a colorful sticky note.

Little rhyme or reason dictated either the order or the similarity of the documents. The pile contained everything from Jillian's divorce papers to her most recent electric bill. A handful of items related to stock and banking were mixed in with the grooming instructions for Snickers, and Ikea furniture construction illustrations.

When she reached the bottom of the stack, her fingers itched. She'd been patiently waiting to dive into one pile above all others. Now that the basic work was complete, she made a space directly in front of her and picked it up. She gave it the place of honor, using her fingers to straighten the edges.

After putting the papers in order by date from oldest to newest, she started with the first sheet. Each piece of paper held a printed email with the same two names featured as sender and recipient. Sometimes the to and from were reversed, but the communication was essentially the same. The emails between Jillian and her son were riddled with anger and pain and peppered with love and regret.

Why Jillian printed and kept these emails wasn't entirely clear except for the general theme, they all involved the same subject—Jillian's will. The seven short messages were all sent during a four-day period this past spring.

May 13
From: Jillian
To: Mike

I updated my will. I've attached the latest copy. The

changes don't really affect you. They are mostly about the charities that get the company shares. You still get all the cash. Just thought you should know.

Love, Mom

May 14
From: Mike
To: Jillian

Mom,
I appreciate that you left me all the cash, but Tina really wants the house.

-Mike

May 14
From: Jillian
To: Mike

I love you. But I want to remind you that you agreed to the terms of my will before you married Tina.

Love, Mom

May 16
From: Mike
To: Jillian

I know I agreed to honor your original will. But things have changed for me. The salary I make at our family company is way below that of a bunch of strangers grandpa never met. And it doesn't keep up with my expenses.

-Mike

May 16
From: Jillian
To: Mike

Perhaps your wife should get a job, or at the very least learn to live on a reasonable budget. I don't plan on dying anytime soon, son. But when I do, that wife of yours will have blown through all your inheritance before it's even in your bank account.

Love, Mom

May 16
From: Mike
To: Jillian

Mom, stop. I don't want to think about your death, ever. Please don't say things like that.

-Mike

May 16
From: Jillian
To: Mike

Sorry, Baby. I love you.

Love, Mom

Why had Jillian kept this correspondence? Why on paper? Why in her drawer with finances and legal documents?

Lemon couldn't answer these questions. But she could preserve the conversation Jillian had carefully documented. She headed to her printer, determined to make sure this was never lost.

CHAPTER FIFTEEN

Lemon's hand actually shook. The phone vibrated in sync as if she experienced her own personal earthquake. The ringing echoed around her until it finally ended with, "Hello."

"Mike?"

"Yeah?"

"It's Lemon."

"Oh, hi Lemon." Mike's voice shifted from curious to friendly. "How are you?"

"I'm good."

"And Snickers? How's he?"

"Good. Real good. He has a new friend. I took in George's dog, Klee."

"Oh, wow. Yeah. George. I guess you've become a dog parent pretty fast."

Lemon rubbed her palm against her knee. "Yeah. Pretty shocking, huh?" She flinched. "I mean, I guess I'm still processing it."

"You're not wrong. Even for a big city this is all pretty crazy." Mike cleared his throat. "So, what can I do for you?"

"I wanted to ask you about your mom's will."

"Oh, yeah. At the reading they said the dog went with the house, which means he would go to Nancy. So I guess I didn't really have the right to give him to you."

"It's okay. I already talked to Nancy. Turns out she didn't want him." She glanced at Snickers, but his self-esteem didn't seem to be damaged by the words. At least that's the impression she got by the dog's posture—lying flat on his back, legs in the air, head turned to the side, tongue out.

"I'm glad you talked to Nancy about it. I'm sorry I didn't call you as soon as I realized."

"It's no problem. I was wondering about the house, to tell you the truth."

"What about it?"

"Well." Lemon's wheels turned as she attempted to channel Mei. "I was looking for some paperwork I thought might be in the house." She flinched as she lied. "You know, for Snickers. And found out that Nancy inherited it, not you, and I was curious about that."

"Then why didn't you call Nancy?" Mike's voice turned stiff and robotic.

Lemon swallowed. She rubbed her palm on the couch because it was too sweaty for her knee. "What is your relationship with Nancy?" Lemon closed her eyes in terror at what she'd said, even as the last words left her mouth.

"Nancy?"

"Um, yeah?"

"Lemon, why are you calling, really?"

"I want to find out who killed your mom. I want to find the rest of her and bury her. I want to see her go to a grave that me and Snickers can visit. I want that for me, honestly. And thought you might want that, too."

A deep trench of silence followed her words. Only heavy breathing told Lemon Mike was still with her. "Yeah. I do want that. What do you need to know?"

"Can you tell me anything about your mom's relationship to George Nichols?"

"Sure. Yeah. I can tell you what I know. They were always friendly.

They had similar friends. Went to dinner parties together. You know, they were friends. But then they started this feud over the painting at the museum, and it just took on a life of its own."

"The Roman painting?"

"Yes. The *supposed* Roman paining. Mom thought it was a fake. George thought it was real. That's what they were fighting over."

Lemon pressed her fingers against her temple. "Your mom was convinced the painting is a fake?"

"She was."

"What do you think?"

"About the painting?"

"Yeah."

"I don't know," Mike said. "I've never seen it."

"Do you know why she thought it was a fake?"

Mike let out a deep breath. "To be honest, I haven't been very attentive to my mom lately. It's not…it's not something I'm proud of. She mentioned it, probably wanting to talk to me about it. We always shared art, but I guess I didn't really make myself available. So…yeah… all I really know is that she thought it was fake. I don't know any of the details."

Lemon's eyes pricked with tears, causing her to blink rapidly. "I appreciate that, Mike. I mean, thanks for the information."

"Sure. Listen," Mike said. "Maybe we can help each other."

Lemon sat at attention, eyes wide. "How?"

"I want to know where my mom is, too. And who killed her. I promise that anything I find out, I'll let you know, if you do the same. Let's keep each other in the loop."

Both and Mei and Jade would be climbing up the walls if they heard this conversation. Neither of them trusted Mike. But regardless of how evil his wife might be, and no matter what her first impressions of the man were, Lemon couldn't believe for one minute that someone who fell to the floor to make friends with a dog was capable of killing his own mother.

"Yeah. I will. I promise."

"Okay. Well, I have to go. Give Snickers a scratch for me."

"Okay. Bye Mike." Lemon disconnected the call. She dropped back into the cushions and tossed her phone beside her.

"Damn," she said. As if he'd heard her, Snickers ran across the hardwood floor, his nails tip-tapping. He jumped up on the couch and pressed his warm, little body into Lemon's thigh. "Thanks buddy." She ran her hand over the pup's fur.

Their temporary peace ended with a text message notification. Lemon threw her head back against the back of the couch and let out a long sigh before reaching for the phone. She cleared the blur from her eyes and glanced at the screen.

The message from Jade couldn't possibly be timelier, or more ominous. *Hey, did you get my DM?*

Lemon bit her lip. *Sorry. Haven't checked socials.*

Jade's long reply came quickly. *Mike Ross was down at my work yesterday. He said hi to me. I asked him if I could tell you I saw him and he said yes—that's CYA thing for me. He went into my colleague's office. She does walk-in fingerprinting and DNA tests. That's all I can say. Don't trust him.*

Lemon swung the van into the only remaining parking spot in the lot. Because it was empty of dogs for the moment, it was a lot easier to maneuver. An early start and a few client cancellations made it possible for Lemon to take a rare midday break and visit Mei at the museum.

Lemon strode through the courtyard, waving to Rodin's masterpiece as she passed the imposing statue. She swung open the gold and glass doors and moved through the lobby dotted with tourists.

Kathy, one of the Guest Services people, waved to her from the Membership booth. Lemon passed the ticket-takers, both of whom recognized her, and headed through the long, grand galleries. Sneaking past some of the greatest art through the ages never ceased to create a tingling in Lemon's mind, as if just being near such magnificence triggered her synapses to fire.

The scent of age matched the cracks in the art that spread like tiny spider webs across the paint in larger patterns as the works grew older. She slipped from the eighteen century into the seventeenth, then the sixteenth. By the time the Renaissance morphed into the dark ages, she was nearly to the end of the long wing.

Tucked in the back, dark and mysterious, were two rooms—one featured artifacts from ancient Rome, the other Ancient Egypt—the domain of the antiquities team. Lemon's pace slowed. A gate blocked the threshold. A laminated sign hung off the metal bars depicting a graphic of a cartoon man in overalls painting a wall accompanied by the words "new exhibit under construction."

Lemon waited, her eyes roaming a massive painting of an iconic religious scene. She took in the subtle colors and the extreme attention to detail. It didn't take long for Mei to appear, her sweet smile showing through the gate's diamond-shaped pattern..

"Hi," Lemon said.

"Oh, my God. You made it!"

Lemon pressed her hand to her chest. "Are you saying you thought I would ask to stop by and then ghost you?"

Mei grinned as she turned a key in the lock and slid the gate open. "I mean, it *has* happened."

Lemon stepped through the opening, moving out of the way so Mei could slide the gate shut. "Once—because Milo fell asleep and wouldn't wake up and he was too damn heavy to move—I had to cancel. And that was for lunch."

Mei threw an arm around Lemon's shoulders. "Okay. I hold grudges."

"You'll get over it. Someday."

Mei led Lemon away from the gate, into the bowels of the large room. "I am very excited to show you this new exhibit."

"I get the extra special preview, huh?"

"Yep, a good week before we do the members-only preview. But, to be honest, we have a parade of friends and family of the employees coming in to checking it out. This exhibit is *super* special."

"I can't wait."

But Mei did make her wait. She showcased the entire Roman exhibit, from the frescos to the marble statues. Until finally, she gripped Lemon's shoulders and turned her toward the wall. "And there it is."

Lemon had seen pictures of the Mona Lisa dwarfed on a huge wall and surrounded by glass. This painting, too, looked as if it would be quite at home above a couch. But it was afforded the largest, most regal space in the room. Where everything else crowded in—huge frescoes and regal statues shuffled together so there was barely space to squeeze between them—this little piece had a great deal of berth.

Not unlike the frescoes, the pale colors hinted at a brighter, more vibrant past. The cracked paint showed its age, completely missing in some places and revealing the stained and yellowed surface beneath it.

"Well, what do you think?" Mei asked.

"It looks really old," Lemon said.

Despite her eyes still being pinned to the painting, Lemon detected Mei's deep sigh. "And?"

Her gaze roamed the painting erratically, moving from one person to another. The people seemed to blend together, their bodies small and entangled in the battle scene. The slash of gold representing a sword or the spray of red illustrating the gruesome results of being hit with such a weapon leapt out at her.

"I mean, it's cool. It's one of a kind, right?"

Mei hung her head for a brief moment. "Yeah. It is."

Lemon spun to face Mei. "I mean it's really great. Millions of dollar's worth of amazing."

Mei laughed. "Come on, let me show you the new stuff in the Egypt room. I know you like that better."

Lemon rubbed her hands together. "You know me well. Mummies

and gods with the head of a jackal. Now *that's* interesting."

They crossed the threshold that separated the two ancient cultures and plunged into a dark space punctuated not with muted colors, but gold and polished stone. Lemon took in a long breath through her nose, which was tickled with the blend of bronze, rock, and death.

Lemon's pace slowed. She took note of every new object, carefully cataloguing each one. The ominous figure of Anubis stood beside the bright and majestic visage of Horus. A huge statute of Osiris served as a delightful centerpiece for the room.

In the very back, at the furthest end of the museum, stood an object Lemon recognized. She moved toward it like a child to a favorite toy. "It's still here!"

"Yes," Mei said. "Of course. We're not big on taking the only sarcophagus we own off exhibit."

Lemon twisted her fingers together, preventing them from reaching out to stroke the surface. "It's so…"

"Yeah, it is. But it's also a heavy mother."

"Well, yeah, it's made of stone. Probably doesn't help that there's a body in there either."

"There's no body," Mei said.

Lemon raised her brows in surprise, a sense of betrayal slamming into her. "No body?"

"There never was. We're not sure if the mummy was removed or if it was a sarcophagus that was made but never filled. At any rate, there is no mummy."

Lemon frowned. "That's a little disappointing."

Mei laughed. "Maybe for you. I'd have to preserve the mummy, and I'm okay with not doing that." Mei turned her away from the granite masterpiece. "Come to my office before you head home, I want to show you the grand opening invitations. They look so good."

Mei and Lemon weaved through the artifacts, back toward a inconspicuous inlet that led to a small suite of offices that included Mei's workspace. But before they reached the sharp turn, Ron Killian stormed out. He stopped in front of them as if he were expecting a salute.

"Mei, what's going on here?"

Mei craned her neck in a move she seemed accustomed to and looked up at her boss. Lemon followed her gaze. Ron's height was somehow exaggerated in this space filled with statues. His blond hair and bright blue eyes stood out among the muted tones of the room. "I was just showing Lemon the new exhibits."

Ron's gaze slid to Lemon but did not soften. They shifted back to Mei before he spoke. "We've had a lot of family and friend sneak peeks lately. There won't be anyone left in the city who hasn't seen it before the grand opening."

"Well, one last one for me," Mei said, her tone still bright.

Ron turned his entire torso toward Lemon and glared at her. "You didn't take any pictures, did you?"

"No. Absolutely not."

"You still walking Milo today?" His tone, still stiff, softened just the tiniest bit.

"Yes, I'm headed to get him now actually."

Ron's head bobbed in a quick, sharp nod. Then he stepped to the side, clapped his heels violently on the hardwood floor and stalked off toward the Egypt room.

Lemon glanced over at Mei. "He's in a bad mood."

"He's been like that for weeks. It makes no sense. We're about to unveil his biggest accomplishment, and he's been acting like he has a stick up his ass."

"Maybe he's just nervous about the grand opening. Plus, two of his board members were murdered. I mean, that is a little stressful."

Mei pressed her finger to her lips. "We literally don't talk about it here. It's like a completely banned subject." She ushered Lemon through the hallway into her cramped office space.

The age of the building provided privacy that few newer ones did. No matter how small the room, they all had doors. Even Mei's "lowest person on the totem pole" status afforded her a quiet place. She took advantage of it, pushing Lemon into her desk chair, shutting the door behind her and leaning against it.

"It's super weird around here," Mei said.

"I can't say I'm surprised. It's super weird around San Francisco in general. It's super weird period. And the museum is kind of at the center of it all."

"Oh, it so is. We have reporters calling all the time. And sometimes they come in pretending to be just looking at art and then they see a staff person and attack. I tell you, I'm terrified going past that gate."

Lemon rubbed her thumb against the smooth arm of Mei's office chair. "But next week you open the exhibit. What will you do then?"

"Hide back here as much as possible. Or in the archives. Thank God I'm not front of house staff. Those poor people."

"Well, that sucks. I'm sorry for all of you. I really am."

Mei sighed. "I'm sorry. You shouldn't feel bad for us. Our problems are nothing compared to yours. You're far more entangled in all of this than any of the staff at the museum. I'm the one who's sorry. I shouldn't be complaining to you, of all people."

Mei's statement hit Lemon with the force of that sarcophagus lid slamming down on her. As much as she wanted to pretend none of this was happening, it was inescapable. Lemon was steeped in it.

CHAPTER SIXTEEN

Tilly leapt into Lemon's lap and regally presented her chin for a scratch. Lemon worked her fingers into the thick fur. The small dog leaned into her touch.

"How's life with two dogs?" Nancy asked, placing a cup of tea into Lemon's free hand.

"Mildly chaotic, but also wonderful."

"Are they getting along better?"

"Thankfully, yes. I think Klee has accepted Snickers as the ruler of the house. And once he did that, he started to be really proud of his job as second-in-command."

Nancy chuckled. "If Snickers is the president and Klee is the vice-president, where does that leave you?"

"I think I'm the secretary of getting dinner."

"Sounds about right." Nancy burst into laughter.

Lemon's shoulders shook, causing her tea to slosh over the side of the cup. Unhappy with the movement, Tilly dropped off Lemon's lap. As she scurried across the floor toward her fluffy, pink bed, she shot a dirty look over her shoulder before collapsing in a heap with a dissatisfied sigh.

"It's good to laugh," Lemon said.

"Ugh. I know." Nancy wiped at her eyes. "Finally tears from laughter instead of grief."

Lemon's heart ached. "It's been hard on you."

Nancy's lips turned up in a sad smile. "Jillian and I were close."

"I know."

"Not really."

"Oh?"

Nancy took three deep breaths, inhaling through her nose and exhaling through pursed lips. "Jillian and I were lovers."

Lemon couldn't be certain if San Francisco was, at that moment, being hit with an earthquake, or if it was simply her own world whose fault lines shifted. As a bisexual woman, Lemon tried to never make assumptions. She understood the damage they could do. But somehow she got caught up in that herself. She'd known Jillian and Nancy for just a few months now, and she erroneously made an assumption about them both.

"You know I'm queer, right?" Lemon said.

Nancy smiled. "I do. I wasn't keeping it from you, dear. I'm just used to discretion." Something about Lemon's expression must have triggered further explanation, because Nancy took another deep breath. "I know. I know. We live in San Francisco. The truth is…our secret…it was really about Mike."

"Mike?" A tingle ran down Lemon's spine.

"Jillian and I shifted from friends to lovers just after her divorce. She moved into the house next to mine, which I owned at the time and sold to her. We might have moved in here together, but we were thinking about Mike. And also, we're opposites. Sometimes it's best for opposites to live apart, you know what I mean?"

"Sure." Lemon smiled. "I know what you mean."

"She did tell Mike about me, not long after the divorce." Nancy took a sip of tea and stared at her mug. "Mike was young and it didn't go well. We didn't break up. But we became discrete, for Mike's sake."

Lemon's frown tugged on her emotions as much as it did her cheeks.

"We'd both been married to men. We'd both been in society. We'd never really been open about our attraction to women. But neither of us was opposed to coming out of the closet, together, for each other." Nancy paused to take another delicate sip of her tea. "But her son trumps everything. And I certainly couldn't argue with that."

"So Mike didn't like your relationship?"

"Not for a long time, no. He came around slowly, very slowly. She was patient, and I tried to be. When she left me the house in her will a couple years ago, he threw a fit. It was some sort resurgence of his anger. I was pretty sure it had to do with his new wife. But Jillian was still infinitely patient with him. And it *did* work out. About six or seven months ago, Mike came over to her house one night—without his wife— and had dinner with both of us. He was all the way there. He accepted our relationship and told Jillian he just wanted her to be happy."

"What happened to change his mind?" Lemon asked.

Nancy shrugged. "I never did find out. I even asked him that night. But he didn't tell me. I don't know if Jillian ever found out either. We didn't talk about it. We were just glad that Mike was in a better place. We were talking about being more public—at least with our friends—when she died."

Lemon leaned forward, elbows on knees. "Do you think Jillian's murder has anything to do with George's?"

Nancy's nostrils flared. She leaned back into the couch as if she were trying to get as far away from Lemon as she could. "Of course not."

"No?"

Nancy's tone turned cold. "No. Why would it?"

"Well, they both served on the Legion board. And I just wondered…" Lemon hesitated beneath Nancy's withering glare. "Maybe it's a dumb idea."

Nancy stood suddenly. "I think you're in shock." Her voice warmed. "You've had two clients die in less than a month. It's a lot." She took a few steps forward, stopping directly in front of where Lemon sat. "You should talk to someone, Lemon. Get some support."

Lemon nodded and stood, taking the cue. "Yeah. I'll do that."

Nancy dropped a hand on Lemon's shoulder. "I have a great therapist.

I'll email you her details, okay?"

"Thanks."

"Sure." Nancy turned Lemon toward the door, making her desire to be alone clear.

"Okay." Jade wiped the grocery list off Lemon's whiteboard. "Let's start with what we absolutely know."

Lemon glared at Snickers and Klee. The two pups snuggled up together on one dog bed, staring wide-eyed at their new pet parent. She blamed them for being the cause of her losing the grocery list. If it weren't for them, she'd be at Jade's apartment now, where there were probably a slew of empty whiteboards just waiting to be used for crime mapping purposes.

Klee yawned, his long tongue curling out into space. Snickers panted, his open mouth forming a smile. She had no choice but to forgive them. Lemon sighed.

Jade wrote the word "museum" on the board. "Okay, Lemon, what time did you see George Nichols at the museum?"

"It was around two," Lemon said.

"Okay." Jade wrote two o'clock under the word museum. "Did anyone else see George alive after that?"

"Yes," Mei said. "He went to the office of his company, Locktite Trust. We know that because the receptionist there told me she saw him come in around two-thirty and leave at five."

"How the hell did you get that info?" Jade asked.

Mei smiled. "The receptionist is queer, and I'm charming. Any more questions?"

Lemon rested her chin on her palm. "Figures."

"It's useful," Jade said. "Good work."

Mei beamed.

"Okay, so five o'clock he leaves his office." Jade's lower lip disappeared behind her front teeth as she recorded the information. "Anything after that?"

"Not from me," Lemon said. "As far as I could tell he never came back to the house that day. Everything was as I left it."

"And how many times were you there, three, right?"

Lemon rubbed her forehead. "Yeah. I picked up Klee and his paperwork. Then after our walk I dropped Klee off. Then when I hadn't heard from George I went back and got Klee and went to the police station."

"Wait. Hold up." Mei threw her arms out as if she were trying to stop traffic. "I thought Klee was a morning dog? Why would you be picking him up after two?"

Lemon brought up the picture of her weekly calendar in her mind. "I did an evening walk that night. And Klee has a standing appointment for all evening walks. And also, George mentioned it when I saw him at the museum. He wanted to make sure I was still taking Klee on the evening walk, and he said he wouldn't be there when I got to the house but to take the envelope of stuff he left for me."

Jade slammed her hands on the counter, the dry erase marker clacking against the granite. "What time did you get the dogs for evening walk that night?"

Lemon's throat tightened. The intensity riding on her answer created a block she had to push past to speak. If she were wrong it would throw everything off. Her memory was great, but the frequency with which she checked a clock was not. "Six. I started picking up dogs at six. I got to George's house probably between ten after and quarter after."

"Okay, just to be perfectly clear," Jade said, once again brandishing her marker. "George was seen leaving his office at five, right?" She pointed to Mei, who nodded. Jade shifted her finger to Lemon. "And he told you he wouldn't be home when you came to pick up his dog sometime after six, right?" Lemon nodded. "So, George must have had plans to be somewhere that evening."

"I mean maybe," Lemon said.

"No maybe about it," Mei said. "He was probably planning to meet someone."

"Or he was just planning to go grocery shopping or something," Lemon said.

Mei and Jade both shot Lemon a look that said they weren't fond of her tame alternatives.

"Okay, so," Jade looked over the board. "He goes to meet someone at five. That's the killer. The person who was going to meet him that night."

"Maybe not," Lemon said. "Maybe he met someone, they had dinner or something, and then someone else killed him."

"That does seem like a possibility," Mei said.

"No," Jade said. "It's not, because a guy who owns the boat that is kept near George's at the marina saw George's boat leaving the marina when he got there at six."

"Oh, my God. That means he was killed between five and six o'clock?" Mei asked.

"Yes. Jade snapped the cap on the marker and threw it on the counter. "And I'm guessing the police have figured that out as well—though I technically don't know that for sure."

"Could he have been killed on the boat?" Mei asked.

"No. He couldn't. That I know. Can't say how, I just do."

"Okay you can't tell us something you know from work. I get that. So, let's focus on what we can know. Someone kills him in the middle of the city and transfers his body to his boat. That seems pretty far-fetched," Lemon said. "Where does someone kill a person in the middle of San Francisco?"

"In a car. In a car in a dark alley," Mei suggested.

"But it was still light out at that time. How do you get the body into the boat?"

Lemon shifted her focus between the two women. Jade lowered her gaze. Mei chewed on her lip. Lemon could almost hear the wheels turning. Hers were too, and she'd come to a conclusion. "Doesn't seem real plausible to me."

"Put them in a gear box." Jade shouted suddenly. Her voice still held excitement even as she lowered the volume to continue. "Put them in a big box and drag or wheel it onto the boat. I've seen people load their boats with some really big shit."

"Me, too," Mei said. "My Uncle Lee has a boat, and I swear some of the stuff he loads on there ought to capsize the thing."

"Was a big box found on the boat?" Lemon asked.

After a long beat, Jade shook her head. "Doesn't mean the killer didn't take it off before setting the boat up to drive out on its own."

"What?" Lemon and Mei spoke in unison.

Jade paled. "Oops."

"I'm guessing you're not supposed to say that."

"No. I'm not supposed to know it. I didn't process the boat. But someone might have mentioned it. It was pretty ingenious really. But I definitely can't tell you about that."

"Okay," Mei said, pressing her fingertips together. "The killer murders him somewhere quiet, puts him in a container. Loads the container into his boat. Takes him out and leaves him on the floor of the boat. Sets the boat to drive itself out into the Bay, and leaves with the container. All in an hour."

"Yep," Jade said.

Maybe Lemon watched too many true crime shows but she started to envision it. A picture formed in her head. "A van. It would work if you had a van."

"Holy shit, yes," Mei said. "You pick him up in a van. Kill him in the van, and put the body in a container, all in the van or like delivery truck, that would work, too."

"Like a U-haul?" Jade asked.

"Sure," Mei said. "Or like the converted van we use to do education at the schools. We have one, the Marine Mammal Center has one. Hell, there's a bunch in the city. They're huge, and designed to carry massive containers of stuff."

"Okay," Lemon said. "The idea of a person being murdered in an education van is totally creeping me out,"

"Me too," Jade said. "And that's saying a lot given what I do for a living."

"What we do now?" Mei asked.

Jade flashed them both a wicked grin. "We check alibis."

CHAPTER SEVENTEEN

Two bottles of wine didn't facilitate the conversation. "We need to settle on a list of suspects so we can check their alibis," Jade said for the third time, wine sloshing in her glass as she gestured wildly.

"Okay. Okay," Mei said, straightening her spine, a nearly impossible task because of the curve of Lemon's overstuffed couch. After her attempt, she ended up slumped back into a slouch in seconds.

Jade pushed up on her toes, creating a gentle motion on the old, wooden rocking chair. "Let's start with the easiest one, someone we can all agree on, and we can go from there."

Warmth spread through Lemon and draped her anxiety in a smooth, alcoholic numbness. One side of her mouth ticked up. "Oh, really? Who is that?"

The rocking chair stopped cold and Jade stared at Lemon's mouth. "You are hot when you smirk."

Beside her, Mei slapped Lemon's knee. She ignored it, tucking herself further into the couch and keeping her gaze on Jade. "Who, then?" she pressed.

"Tina Ross," Jade said. "She hated Jillian. No question about that."

"According to my mom, wanting to kill your mother-in-law is common," Lemon said. "But a little extreme to be the only motive."

"But it's not the only motive," Mei said. "Tina was furious that Mike didn't get a better job at the company, and she must have known Mike was going to inherit something when Jillian died."

Jade jumped in. "She kills her husband's mother out of a mix of revenge and greed?"

Lemon stuck one finger in the air as if she were on an old detective show. "But then how does she do all that? Kill Jillian? Cut off her feet? Hide the body somewhere no can find? And does that mean she also killed George? Because if so, I have a whole new set of questions."

"Okay, let's take the two murders separately first," Jade suggested. "If Tina did kill Jillian, she needed help. I won't argue with that. But I think her accomplice is obvious."

Lemon tapped her fingers against her knee. The feeling rising in her breast reminded her of the time she defended Amber Gwin, her first girlfriend, from a pair of bitchy bullies. "Not Mike." Her tone made her statement definitive. No argument to be had.

Mei wasn't the least bit intimidated by Lemon's resolve. "Yes, Mike. Think about it. Passed over by his mother, brainwashed by his wife, unhappy with his lot in life."

"He's not going to participate in the murder of his own mother. No way."

"You watch as much true crime as I do," Mei said. "You know that it *does* happen."

"I've talked to this man. I've...I feel like on some level we kind of connected. And I'm telling you, he's not capable of matricide." A rising tide of sympathy for Mike had slowly overtaken her, and now the truth came out.

"Okay." Jade reached across the canyon of space between them and stroked two fingers over Lemon's knee with a light touch. "We hear you. So, if it's Tina, she either acted alone or got help from someone else. Can we agree on that?"

"Yeah, okay," Mei conceded.

"So." Jade leaned back and slapped her hand on her thigh. "Let's talk about other suspects."

"Nancy." Mei's voice clapped through the room like thunder.

"I object." Lemon's response hit the walls just as hard and echoed around them.

Mei leaned forward, making the couch cushion she perched on rub against the one Lemon occupied. She poured a stream of wine into all three glasses on the table. "Are you going to object to everyone?"

A petulance Lemon rarely allowed to surface grabbed hold of her. She picked up her newly filled glass of wine, sank back into the couch and crossed her legs. "Possibly."

"Okay, well, let me make my case first," Mei said.

"I'd like to hear this, too." Jade mirrored Lemon's posture. "She's not really on my list, to be honest."

"You gotta ask yourself, why did Jillian leave her house to Nancy. I mean, they were best friends sure. And I love you, Lemon. But if I had a kid and you were already all set, I'd totally leave my kid the house, you know."

Lemon raised an eyebrow at Mei. "What does that have to do with murder?"

"Money, greed, murder. All tied together. That house is worth a lot of money, whether you sell it or rent it out or whatever," Mei said.

"So," Jade said, "even though—as you already pointed out—Nancy is set for money, she kills her best friend for more money. I'm not buying it. But." Jade turned her gaze on Lemon. "I have to wonder why was Jillian leaving her house to Nancy, especially since Nancy is older and by all rights might have died first."

"I imagine they both did the same thing, leaving their houses to each other," Lemon said.

"Wait," Mei said. "It's like a freaking Christmas present? Nancy has no one to leave her house to so she leaves it to Jillian, who in turn leaves her house to Nancy? I mean, that's nice when it comes to fruitcake but we're talking about prime San Francisco real estate here."

"There's a little more to it than that," Lemon said. "And when I tell you, you'll take her off your suspect list."

Jade rocked forward. "Let's have it then."

"Nancy and Jillian were a couple." The words landed as Lemon suspected they would, like a bomb exploding in her tiny living room.

"What? Really?" Mei asked.

"Seriously?" Jade said. "I did not see that coming."

"Neither did I," Lemon admitted. "I guess we're bad queers."

"Holy shit," Jade said. "Nancy might be off your list, but she just went *on* mine."

"What? Why?" Lemon asked.

"The significant other is *always* the first one you have to suspect."

"No way. Not this time. Not Nancy. Come on." Lemon's voice morphed into a gentle whine. "Why?"

"They were a secret, right? Whose idea was that?" Jade asked.

Lemon blew out a breath. "Jillian. But only because of her son. He didn't really approve. And Jillian wanted to try to preserve her relationship with him after the divorce. I mean, it's complicated."

"Yes. It's complicated. And so are the feelings of a partner who is kept locked in a closet. Believe me, I've been there." Jade's face fell at the end of her statement, as if she'd been caught in a rainstorm.

"I'm sorry." Lemon kept her gaze locked to Jade's striking blue eyes.

Jade's melted smile quirked back up on one side. The crooked expression traveled into Lemon's heart. "It's fine. I'm just saying. Nancy can't be ruled out, especially in light of this information."

Lemon deflated. She meant for this information to clear Nancy, push her name right off the whiteboard of suspicion. Instead, her efforts failed them both. "Let's move on. There are other suspects. What about Hayley? Or even George?"

"Let's tackle George first," Jade suggested.

"Well," Mei said. "He's dead. So there's that."

"Doesn't mean he couldn't have killed Jillian before he himself was killed." Lemon nestled her wine glass in her lap. "I mean, perhaps he killed Jillian and someone else killed him in revenge."

"It's not a bad theory," Jade conceded. "But then who killed him?"

"Mike," Mei suggested.

"Wait. This is kind of bullshit." Lemon set her wineglass on the coffee table hard enough that a splash of red liquid landed in a perfectly round bubble on the glass surface. "He's either evil enough to participate in his own mother's murder or he loves his mom so much he'd kill for her. Which is it?"

Mei shrugged. "I don't know. Could be either. I'm just pointing out all the possibilities here."

"Okay." Jade held up her half-empty glass wine. "If George killed Jillian, who else could have killed him?"

Neither Lemon nor Mei moved.

"I'll tell you," Jade said. "Nancy. Nancy could have gotten revenge for Jillian's death."

"She couldn't physically get his body on that boat," Lemon pointed out. "And she wouldn't be able to program the boat to drive itself. Believe me, I'm the one who showed her how use Facebook."

"She had help." Jade took a sip of wine. "It's just one theory."

"What about Hayley?" Lemon asked. "Something weird happened between her and Jillian. Something that ended her employment. It could have been motive for murder."

"Not denying it," Jade said. "But even if she actually killed Jillian over that, why would she kill George?"

Mei stuck her hand up as if she were waiting to be called on by the teacher but was too impatient to actually be given permission to speak. "Because he holds Jillian's trust money. If she wanted to kill Jillian over money, it follows that she would kill George for the same reason."

"Exactly!" Lemon said.

Jade frowned. "It's a good argument. But I have to admit to having a hard time seeing Hayley as a murderer."

"Were you able to get any information about her relationship with Jillian out of her?" Mei asked.

Jade's pink lips turned down creating a crease on both sides of her mouth. "'Fraid not. I've tried several times. I even got her drunk one night. But as soon as I would bring up the subject of Jillian, she shut down."

"Who are we missing?" Lemon asked. "I feel like we're missing someone."

"What about one of the other Legion board members?" Jade asked. "We can't ignore that both dead people were on the board. Maybe there was someone else that had a grudge against them both, or wanted to be in charge so they had to take out the president and vice president."

"I don't know much about the other board members, but I can snoop around and find out," Mei said.

"Sounds like a plan," Jade said. She leapt out of the rocking chair, and hustled over to the white board. "So Mei is going to work on the board." Her arm swooped as she recorded the assignment. "And even though I can't get information out of Hayley, I will at least find out where she was between five and six on the day George was killed. We'll find out if she has an alibi so we can eliminate her or not."

"In George's death," Lemon pointed out.

"It's the one we have the tightest timeline for, right?" Jade said.

Lemon knew the timeline for Jillian's disappearance was at least six hours, so she couldn't argue with Jade's logic. They would start with alibis for George's murder and go from there. "Okay, yeah. I'll get alibis from Mike and Nancy."

"If they have them," Mei said.

Lemon's mind buzzed. They would have alibis. They had to.

Lemon dropped Snickers at Mei's feet. The little dog immediately ran to the end of his fifteen-foot leader, stopped just short of yanking himself into an awkward harness dance, and bent into a "C" shape to poop.

"Nice, Snickers. I hope you're a little more charming when Marabel comes," Mei said.

"Leave him alone. He doesn't know what we're doing here anymore than I do," Lemon said. "What *are* we doing here? And who is Marabel?"

"First of all, this is a lovely park. I don't know why either of you are complaining. The reviews say it's a great place to take dogs. There's even a leash free area over there." Mei pointed to her left.

Lemon lurched as Snickers tested the bounds of his lead. "No, we're good."

"This park also happens to be close to Marabel's house and I arranged for us to meet her here."

"Who is Marabel? Why are we meeting her? And why did I have to bring Snickers?" The trust Lemon had in her best friend carried her far enough to get her to the park with no explanation, but now curiosity consumed her.

Mei's gaze bounced around, then glanced down at the time display on her phone, and finally up to Lemon. She leaned in. "She's on the board, and everyone says she's a huge gossip. If you want to keep a secret, never tell Marabel. Anyway, I kind of accidentally slash purposely ran into her the other day. And I mentioned that my best friend is Snickers' new mom. And apparently she loves Snickers. Or so she said. I made this big deal about how she has to meet up with you to see Snickers, and I didn't let it go until she agreed."

"So, you pressured this woman into a date with a dog?"

Mei straightened and swiveled her head to scan the park again. "Basically, yeah. I figured we could use Snickers as bait to get what we need. Only, she might be flaking." She squinted her eyes as she stared out at the grass speckled with sunlight.

"Well, if she does come, what the hell are we going say?"

"We'll think of something. Guided small talk, you know."

"Actually, no. I'm not so good at it. I brought the dog. The rest is all you."

"You have to admit that you've been doing a pretty good job of weaseling information out of people lately, Lemon. You're putting that Communications degree to good use." Mei nudged Lemon's arm with her elbow. "You're turning into a manipulative extrovert, my friend."

Lemon fully rejected Mei's bizarre label. She bent over to give her attention to Snickers instead. She dropped down to the grass and invited the pup into her lap.

"There she is," Mei said. "Stay here and I'll bring her over."

Lemon kept her focus on stroking Snicker's cotton candy fluff until she could no longer hear Mei's presence. Then she raised her head, squinting into the sun to examine the small woman Mei greeted at the threshold where the grass met the sidewalk.

As they approached, the figure came into clearer focus. Shorter and stouter than Mei, the woman's legs moved quickly to keep up as the pair hustled across the grass. Her blunt haircut bounced in the sunlight.

Lemon moved to get up, but Snickers settled in deeper, seemingly happy to nap in the warmth of the afternoon. As the two women grew close, Lemon saw no choice but to rouse the sleeping pup so she could stand up and greet them. Snickers complied, but rather than stand at her side, he pawed at her shin until she picked him up and held him in her arms.

Lemon tucked him under one arm like a football and sprang to her feet as Mei and Marabel came to a stop in front of them.

"Marabel, this is my friend Lemon, the one I told you about."

The woman cocked her head, her hazel eyes shining. Deep folds radiated out from them, showing her age, which Lemon guessed was as much as a decade more than Nancy. "Hello, Lemon. What a beautiful name."

"Thank you, ma'am. It's a pleasure to meet you."

"I used to know someone with a girl named Lemon. We were in a group together a few years back."

"Um, I don't suppose it was Lilly Lister."

Marabel's face lit up brighter than the sun hitting her wire-framed glasses. "Yes. Is she your mother?"

Lemon attempted to nod, but Marabel's body halted her motion as she threw herself at Lemon in an aggressive hug. "Oh Goodness. It's nice to meet you." Marabel pulled back and looked down at Snickers, who had given a whine of protest when the women squished them in the center of the embrace. "Your mother is a wonderful woman. And there's Snickers!" Pulling her hands away from Lemon, she clapped them together. "I have such great memories of Jillian, in so many of them, Snickers was at her side, or in her purse." She giggled like a giddy, young girl then quickly morphed it into a sad sigh. "Such good times."

"Tell us about Jillian," Mei prompted.

Marabel reached out one hand, presenting it to Snickers. The pup pulled his nose out of the nestle of Lemon's elbow and carefully stretched toward the offered appendage. The leathery, black nose quivered as it investigated. The scent must have triggered Snicker's memory because he pushed his head into Marabel's palm.

Marabel smiled as she stroked the tan and white fluff on Snicker's head. "She was a good person. People would never call her sweet or soft and fuzzy like her dog. But that doesn't make her any less good."

"Like how?" Mei cocked her head to one side.

"Oh, you know. She used her talents to make things better. She was always like that. She took her family business and used her intelligence and savvy to grow it and make it even more successful. And she used her intense drive and passion to support the causes she volunteered for. And no matter what they say about her, she cared deeply about people. Her son, her fellow volunteers, everyone. She wasn't a misanthrope."

"Did someone actually say that?" Mei asked. "That Jillian was a misanthrope?"

Marabel's focus shifted. She pulled her hand away from Snickers and shoved it in her pocket. Her bright eyes turned on Mei with a new sparkle. "Oh people definitely said that, especially her enemies."

"Enemies. Wow. I can't imagine Jillian having enemies. Can you, Lemon?"

Murder was fresh in Lemon's mind again, not because they were talking about Jillian, who was murdered, but because Mei brought Lemon into this insane ruse and then shoved her into the center of the dance floor. "Um. No. Not really."

"Well, she had them." A soft groan emitted from Marabel's throat.

"Like George Nichols?" Mei asked.

Marabel's eyes narrowed, crinkling the skin even further, the crow's feet shooting back to her hairline. "Where did you hear that?"

Mei kept her composure, the calm, cool exterior never wavering. "It's a pretty common rumor around the museum."

Marabel's gaze slid up and down Mei quickly as if she were making a clinical assessment of this person in front of her. "How long have you worked at the museum, young lady?"

"Going on four months," Mei replied.

"Well, if you'd been around longer, you'd know that wasn't always the case." Marabel stuck her hands on her hips. "They were close friends once. It was Jillian who recruited George to the Legion board, and it was Jillian who nominated him for vice president. She handpicked George to be her successor. Does that sound like an enemy to you?"

"No ma'am, it sure doesn't." Mei batted her eyes. "That's what makes it so perplexing that everyone is saying that now. Don't you think?"

Marabel's hands dropped to her sides. Her eyes opened and her mouth grew softer. "Yes." One eyebrow and one side of her mouth quirked up simultaneously as if they were attached to one another with an invisible string. "It might seem perplexing to an outsider."

Mei's genius hit Lemon like a light bulb thrown at her head. She led this woman, this virtual stranger, to a place where she would want to spill what she knows. A heady combination of defensiveness and pride wound a short path to their goal.

"But," Marabel shifted closer to Mei, seeming to have forgotten about Snickers and Lemon altogether, which was just fine with both of them. Snickers flirted with sleep, and Lemon was too terrified to mess up Mei's magic to speak. "What you probably don't know is that they had a falling out."

"Really?" Mei's entire body leaned into the act. Her eyebrows kissed her hair, her mouth gaped open, and her body arched toward Marabel. "What kind of falling out?"

"It was over a painting. A painting in your department." Marabel stuck her finger at Mei, pressing into her sternum for a brief moment before pulling it back and smirking.

"No way."

Marabel nodded and ended the action with her chin stuck so high she had to look down to see Mei. "Oh yes, the very picture that is being dedicated to George next weekend at the special exhibit."

"You don't mean the Roman?" Mei's fake question sounded so real, Lemon herself almost forgot that Mei knew all about this already.

"Oh yes, sweetheart. Jillian and George fought over that thing since Ron first brought it to their attention. The first time I ever saw those two really go at it. I mean, I'd seen them argue. Everyone argues about things they are passionate about. Nearly everyone on the board has had a pet project they went to battle for at some point in time. But this was different. I swear there were times I thought they would come to blows."

"Wow. Why was it so contentious?"

"Jillian wanted another appraiser to take a look at it before they bought it, a friend of hers. But they'd already had an appraiser look at it and they all agreed that it was genuine and worth what we were paying for it. George thought it was a waste of time to get another opinion. And he was in a huge hurry to get it on display."

"I have to say, I'm surprised Jillian didn't win, though," Mei said. "People say she's kind of a force to be reckoned with."

"There's no doubt about that," Marabel agreed. "But she was at a disadvantage because we have this conflict-of-interest rule. A board member can't suggest hiring someone they have a personal or professional relationship with. If the person is to be hired by the museum another, unaffiliated board member has to bring it to a vote before the board."

"So why didn't Jillian get someone else to suggest hiring her appraiser friend."

Marabel pointed at Mei. "Oh, if only it were that easy. See, her friend is Lucas Johns."

"Oh," Mei said. "I see."

Lemon didn't. "See what?"

Both women turned to her as if they'd just remembered her presence. "Lucas Johns does a lot of work locally," Mei said.

"He's does work for every art collector in this town," Marabel added. "And that includes everyone on the board—except George."

"So, George was the only one who could bring it to a vote to have this Lucas Johns person appraise the painting?" Lemon asked.

"That's right," Marabel said. "And now he's dead."

CHAPTER EIGHTEEN

Book club ended on a high note. Hayley was literally the only person who actually made it to the end of the book—probably the only one to make it past chapter three if any of them had been honest instead of blatantly lying. And that's what had caused the high note. They'd completely abandoned any pretense of discussing the book and opened several bottles of wine.

With Ubers called and slurred goodbyes, everyone left Hayley's apartment, except Mei, Jade, and Lemon who lingered like poorly disguised secret service agents. Rather than wither beneath the scrutiny, Hayley stepped up to the task of hosting the half-drunk spies with ease.

"Okay, does anyone actually want coffee, or another glass of wine?" Hayley asked.

"Wine," all three echoed at the same time.

Hayley laughed before ducking into the kitchen to retrieve another bottle. When she returned, all three secret agents had plopped onto the couch side-by-side, folding into the thick cushions.

"We have questions," Jade said as soon as Hayley returned with the bottle and filled all the glasses.

Done with her task, Hayley sat gingerly in the loveseat opposite the filled couch. She smiled. "Questions. About what?"

"Well," Jade said. "We want to know what really happened between you and Jillian. She's dead and so is George Nichols. And we need to know the truth."

Hayley took a gingerly sip of her wine. "You're trying to solve the mystery, huh?"

"We are. And we want to know what you know."

Hayley sighed. "You want to know why I quit working with Jillian?"

"Yes," Jade said. "The truth. We *need* it."

Hayley took another long sip before setting the glass on the coffee table. "I figured this was coming. I knew you'd all become involved when Jillian died. Then George…it was inevitable. Mind if I smoke?"

"Do what you gotta do. As long as we get the truth," Jade said.

Hayley slid open a drawer in the end table flanking one side of the loveseat. She retrieved a cardboard packet of cigarettes and lighter. After lighting one and taking a long drag, she blew out the smoke like it was stream of gold and smiled. "When I worked for Jillian I thought I knew her. I thought were kind of friends, you know, at least the way an employee and employer can be, or the way two queer women can be." She lifted an eyebrow, her gaze moving from one guest to the next. "No reaction. So you know?"

"That she was in a relationship with Nancy, yeah," Mei said.

Hayley nodded. "They were a couple. Only reason they weren't completely public was because of Jillian's son, Mike." Hayley took another drag and blew the thick, white smoke out her nose, making her look a little like a lesbian dragon about to burn a house of homophobes to the ground. "But in private circles it was well known. They weren't into pretending any more than they had to."

"Did you get along with Nancy?" Jade asked.

"Yeah, sure. I still do. I mean, it's not like we were going to have dinner next week or anything. But I saw her on occasion and we were always friendly, had good conversations about her dog or her house or whatever."

"What about Mike?" Jade asked. "What do you think of him?"

Jade flicked her cigarette violently into a small glass ashtray that looked as if it had been stolen from a local pub back when people could still smoke in pubs. "He's fine other than making his mom live in the closet and marrying a raging bitch."

"Hey," Jade said. "Don't hold back."

"Look, I realize I've been pretty tight-lipped with you all." Hayley took another drag. Slow and drawn out, it seemed to Lemon to be an evasive maneuver. But she did, eventually, get to the point. "But despite what it might look like, I don't like secrets. Especially ones that hurt people. Whether that has to do with keeping a loved one in the closet or cheating on them."

"Cheating?" Lemon shifted forward in her seat, her knee thumping the coffee table and causing her wine glass to shift and slosh dangerously. "What does cheating have to do with anything?"

Hayley mirrored Lemon's actions, pulling herself to the edge of her own seat and setting her elbow on her knee, cigarette in the air, its curl of dirty white smoke rising between them like the fuzz of the camera in an old film. "It's why I quit my job."

"Wait. Confused," Mei said.

"You're not the only one," Jade said.

Hayley stubbed out her cigarette, squishing it as if it were all the feelings inside her. "I found out Jillian was cheating on Nancy. And I was pissed. I have a freaking moral compass, and she broke it. I don't fuck with cheats. Even if it affects my paycheck."

Lemon's spine tingled. This narrative was all wrong. She could feel it. "With who?"

"An employee of all things. I mean, I knew the guy because I wrote him checks. Can you believe that? Sleeping with an employee behind your girlfriend's back. It's so fucking wrong!" Hayley's hand shook as she flipped open the cigarette box to retrieve another smoke.

She wouldn't be giving out much more information. Lemon was certain that they needed to change the subject in the next ninety seconds or Hayley would call them all an Uber on her own app. So Lemon blurted out the one thing she absolutely had to know before they left this conversation behind for good. "What's his name?"

"Lucas Johns," Hayley said before rising from her seat. "Is that all?"

"No, it's not." Jade jumped out of her own seat and met Hayley in the center of the room.

The showdown sent fingers of chill up Lemon's spine. Was she watching a friendship implode before her eyes?

Hayley leaned back on her heels. "Okay. What else do you want?"

Jade's face softened. "An alibi for five to six pm on the eighteenth."

"Wait. The eighteenth? That's not the day Jillian died."

"It's not. It's the day George was killed."

"Ahhh." Hayley clasped her hands together. "So you think whoever killed Jillian also killed George."

"It's one possibility," Jade said. "But we don't have a tight window for when Jillian was killed."

"But you do for George?"

Jade nodded.

"Okay, well. I was at Hamilton and Jackson going over their payroll. I do it for them as a contractor."

Jade took a step back, her hands held out in a peace offering. "Thank you for that."

"Sure. But I'm curious, why do you think the same person killed them both?"

Jade didn't answer Hayley's question, instead she dropped back down on the couch and took a sip of wine. Mei mirrored Jade's actions, leaving only Lemon to respond.

"Coincidence. Occam's Razor." Lemon shrugged.

"So it's the easiest explanation?" Hayley dropped back into her own seat. "I suppose it is. What are the odds that two people who have known each other for years and serve on the same board of directors are both murdered within two weeks of each other? An explanation that there are two unrelated people out there with two different motives seems to be pretty unlikely. So, yeah. I can see that. One killer, or group of killers is responsible for both murders."

"And if that's true," Jade said. "Then gathering alibis could help us narrow down the suspects."

"I was on the list?" Hayley sounded more amused than offended.

Jade shrugged and grinned. "You were being sketchy about your relationship with Jillian. And it doesn't take much to get on the list right now."

Hayley settled into the couch. "Who else is on the list?"

"A few others."

Hayley rolled her eyes. "Fine. You don't want to tell me your list, I accept that. But I hope you have Mike Ross on it."

"Thanks for meeting me. I know it was kinda out of the blue." Lemon shifted her seat so the sun no longer directly penetrated her retinas. The umbrella overhead teased her with tiny morsels of shade that seemed to shift and move until she hit the exact right spot.

Across from her, Mike was bathed in darkness, his eyes wide, smiling. "It's no problem, Lemon. We had a deal."

They did. They promised to keep each other apprised on everything they found out about Jillian's death. But Lemon didn't share that with her partners in crime. They still didn't trust Mike. And that's part of the reason she sat here on a Tuesday afternoon at a crowded outdoor café in the Financial District to discuss Mike's alibi.

The other reason was a mildly easier subject to broach. "Have you ever heard of a man named Lucas Johns?"

Mike jerked his head back. "Yes. Of course. Why do you ask about him?"

"Well." Lemon wondered if she should demand answers first, or tell Mike what she knew? Being a people pleaser, the choice was obvious. "Someone told me they thought your mother was having a romantic relationship with him."

For the first time since she'd met him, Mike laughed. Loud and hard, it created an involuntary warm feeling that spread through Lemon's chest, up her neck and into a broad smile. There was something magical about a good, genuine laugh in the middle of grief. She couldn't help but chase that feeling.

When Mike's mirth died down he stared at her, the same goofy grin on his face planted on hers. "I'm sorry, I'm just struggling to picture them together. No. I'm sure there was no relationship. My mom was in love with Nancy. Really in love.

Lemon smiled. "I believe that. But why would this person believe your mom was having an affair with Lucas Johns?

Mike shrugged and wrapped his hands around his glass of water that dripped with condensation in the early afternoon sun. "I have no idea why anyone would think that. Lucas Johns is an art appraiser she worked with. Their relationship was professional."

"Yeah. I heard he worked for your mom and a lot of other people in town, too."

"Yes. And he's a good guy, and a professional. And he definitely wasn't having an affair with my mom. Who would say such a thing?"

Lemon shifted, causing the plastic slats of her chair to squeak. "I don't really want to say."

Mike sighed. "What about our deal?"

The next words to fly out of Lemon's mouth were the least thought out she'd ever uttered and were followed instantly by instant regret. "And what if you're the killer?"

"Of my own mother?" The horror in Mike's eyes reflected back to her as clear as the afternoon sunshine.

"No. No. Of George."

Mike narrowed his eyes. "That's offensive!"

"You're right. I'm sorry. It's just that I told my friends I would prove it to them. That you aren't a murderer. Because I believe that, Mike. I really do. And that's why I need an alibi from you."

Mike folded his arms. "When?"

"Between five and six in the evening on the eighteenth."

Mike nodded. "A Tuesday, right? I will double-check my calendar, but I was probably at work. I rarely go home before six or seven Monday through Thursday. Chances are good I was at my office and there are plenty of witness. What about you?"

Lemon's brain ground to a halt. "What?"

"What's your alibi for the evening of the eighteenth?"

"I guess that's a fair question."

"I think so."

Lemon swallowed and tried to make her mind function again. Flooded with empathy, she suddenly understood what she'd put Mike through only moments before. There was nothing warm and fuzzy about being accused of murder. "I was walking three dogs at Jefferson Square Park. I must have been seen by at least twenty-five people. I knew two of them, not by name, but by their dog's names. I could find them again if I needed to."

"That's good enough for me." Mike propped his elbows on the wobbly, round table. "So, let's get back to Lucas Johns. Who thinks my mother was having an affair with him, and why?"

"Hayley Kline. She used to be your mom's accountant."

"Yeah. I know who she is." Mike's tone indicated that he liked her about as much as she liked him—which wasn't saying a lot given that Hayley had accused Mike of murder about sixteen hours ago.

"Apparently, while she was working for your mother, she became convinced they were together."

"But why?" Mike asked.

"I guess she caught them being secretive about something. She made assumptions."

"That's pretty flimsy."

"I don't disagree," Lemon said.

"Look. Lucas is a very secretive guy. That's just him. He always acts like his appraisals are classified documents pertaining to the Kennedy assassination. There is a reason everyone uses him, and part of that his discretion. If he and mom were being secretive from her accountant, I can assure you, it had nothing to do with sex." He chuckled. "Honestly."

"Something else nefarious?"

"Unlikely. My mom was an on-the-level person. But she did have trust issues. She and Lucas had that in common. Neither of them would have talked business in front of a contracted employee. No offense."

"None taken," Lemon said. "She didn't talk business in front of me, and I appreciate that. She was always kind though."

Mike sighed. "People always think of my mom as cold. But she really wasn't. She was a nice lady."

"Yeah. She was."

"Okay." Mike's voice echoed loudly in the space, making Lemon's head snap up. "So what do we do to find the asshole who killed her?"

Lemon folded her hands. "Let me ask you this. Do you think the same person killed your mom and George?"

"Yes. I do. And I think the motive was the same, though I don't know what it is right now."

"Me neither. But what you could do is use our alibi timeline with other people you suspect."

"Will do." He held out his hand over the table. "And I'll let you know what I find out. Can I expect the same in return?"

Lemon clasped his large hand. Despite the fact it felt smooth as velvet against Lemon's own leash-shredded one, his grip was strong and firm. "Yes. Absolutely."

CHAPTER NINETEEN

"I am sorry, but we need to have a weird conversation." It was the best way Lemon could think to start off the discussion despite a very sleepless night of running through options in her head.

"Okay." Nancy's smile didn't waver. Relaxed in her recliner, she seemed completely at ease.

Lemon perched on the couch across from Nancy, a warm cup of tea nestled in her hands. "First, where were you between five and six pm on the eighteenth?"

Nancy closed her eyes. She remained still for so long Lemon feared she might have fallen asleep. When her eyes suddenly popped open, Lemon's entire body jumped. "I was here, alone."

"Okay. Thanks."

Nancy trapped Lemon beneath her withering gaze. "Tell me more. How did you narrow down this timeframe?"

Lemon set her tea on the coffee table and twisted her fingers together in complex patterns. "My friends and I have been investigating Jillian and George's murders."

"I see."

Lemon suddenly felt the way she had at eight when her grandmother caught her stealing a cookie from the cocker spaniel shaped ceramic jar that sat on the kitchen counter. "We just want to help."

"I understand that. And I also think it's dangerous." Nancy raised one eyebrow.

As much as this conversation created a roiling in her stomach, Lemon still preferred it to the one they had yet to have about the man her partner may or may not have been cheating on her with. "Dangerous how?"

"Two people are dead. Murdered. There is a person out there willing to kill people to keep their secret. Doesn't it occur to you that maybe you shouldn't go snooping around in that?"

Whatever fear Nancy meant to instill in Lemon fled ahead of the sheer curiosity she awakened. "What secret?"

Nancy pressed her lips together in a disapproving line. "Lemon. Leave this to the police." Lemon met Nancy's gaze. "Promise me."

That wasn't something Lemon could do. And asking about Lucas Johns seemed impossible now. Stuck in a vice of her own making, Lemon was rendered immobile. Should she try to reason with Nancy, explain that something had been lit deep inside her that required she find Jillian's killer? Or should she simply acquiesce, admit that no matter what her heart told her, she was not in a place to be able to solve a murder—or two?

"The thing is…" Having no idea what to say Lemon stalled out mid-sentence. "It's just that…"

Nancy reached across the space between them, her movement quick and unexpected. She grasped Lemon's hand with trembling fingers. "Lemon, listen to me. I talked to Helen McBride today, that's Jillian's lawyer."

"I know. She called me once."

Nancy's eyes were an ocean of bright blue, her lids so wide the irises looked like little worlds floating in a sea of white clouds. "Did she ask you about a document she was looking for?"

Pinpricks ran down Lemon's spine. "Yes."

"Well, she called me looking for it, too."

"Did she…has it been found?"

"No. But someone wants to find it really bad. Helen's office was broken into last night and completely ransacked."

The voice of her grandmother echoed in her mind. *Not everything is about you.* It was a mantra repeated to bother Lemon and her mother every time they worried about something. She pulled that out now, grasping onto what she could only describe as hope. "But maybe it doesn't have anything to do with that letter. I mean, maybe someone else was looking for something else."

Nancy let go of Lemon's hand. She sat straight, hands on her knees. "You are a smart girl, Lemon. You need to think this through. And I'm sure you'll come to the same conclusion Helen and I have. This isn't a coincidence. Nothing was taken from Helen's office, not even from the petty cash drawer. The files were all gone through. There is no doubt in her mind—or mine—that whoever it was that ransacked her office was looking for the letter Jillian left for George. And with both Jillian and George dead, that letter must have something really important in it, something worth killing for. Don't put yourself in the way of a person like that."

Lemon sucked at lying, but comfort she could do well. She reached out across the empty space between them, placing her hand over Nancy's. "As scary as this is, I think it's helpful. The police have more to work with. They'll figure this out and get the killer off the streets. I'm sure of it."

Nancy gave Lemon's hand a squeeze. "I sure hope so, sweetheart. Because I don't think I can take anymore loss."

"Thanks for meeting me." Lemon's face burned fiery with shame. After weeks of intense flirting, she'd gone from nerdy hot to desperate hot mess in seconds flat.

Jade cocked her head, concern shone in her eyes. "Of course, it's no problem."

"But, you're at work."

"And you're in trouble. I'm glad you came to me." Jade's position opposite Lemon at the impossibly clean square table crammed into a tiny, sterile room made it feel as if she were a million miles away.

The bright white walls reflected Lemon's anxiety back to her in the small space. The thick air stuck in her lungs, working her diaphragm overtime to keep oxygen pumping into her body.

"Lemon, what's going on?" Jade placed her hand, palm up, on the table between them.

Lemon pulled her hand out from between her knees and grasped Jade's. "So, do you remember when I told you about Jillian's lawyer calling me?"

Jade nodded, completely focused on Lemon.

"Well, she was looking for a letter that Jillian left for George. And she had given George that letter, but after he died, the police couldn't find it."

"I remember."

"Well, apparently, the attorney, Helen McBride's office was broken into yesterday. Nancy and Helen are convinced the person who broke in was looking for the letter."

Jade used her free hand to stroke her thumb and forefinger across her chin. "Okay. So, what do you know about this letter? Have you ever seen it? Was it ever in your possession?"

"No. Not at all. But Helen called me because she apparently thought I might have it."

"And why did she think that?"

"Because I'd been in the house."

Jade suddenly sat back, her eyes wide. "How did she know that?"

Lemon shrugged. "I guess she just figured it out because she knew I had the dog."

"How? How did she know that, Lemon?"

"I don't know. Why does this matter?"

Jade's intensity washed over the room like a tidal wave. She leaned forward again, with such force she shoved the table an inch closer to Lemon. "It matters. Did she say how she knew you'd been at George's house?"

"No. But I thought it was obvious since I had the dog."

"How did she know you had George's dog?"

"I don't know. I probably told her."

"But she called you thinking—no knowing—that you had been in that house, right?"

Lemon squeezed Jade's hand. "Yeah. So, what's the problem? What's wrong with that?"

"Call her. Call her right now."

"Are you serious?"

"Do you have her number or do you need me to look it up?"

Lemon spent ten seconds staring at Jade before she pulled her phone out of her pocket and placed it on the table. After she hit all the right buttons, the ominous sound of the muffled ringing flooded the space around them.

"McBride Law Offices. This is Melanie speaking. How can I help you?"

"Is Helen available," Lemon asked.

Jade spoke into the phone, her voice unnecessarily loud. "It's Lemon Lister calling. It's important."

"Oh, Ms. Lister. I'm sorry. Ms. McBride is out of the office at the moment. Can I help you with anything?"

"Oh, um, can you just ask her to—"

Jade abruptly interrupted. "Actually, maybe you can help, Melanie."

"Yes. Of course. What can I do for you?"

Lemon glared at Jade. But the withering look didn't stop Jade from pushing onward. "This is a friend of Lemon's. I work at the crime lab. And I was wondering if you would know how Ms. McBride knew that Lemon Lister was in possession of George Nichols's dog."

A long pause pulled at the room, the silence from the phone deafening. "Well, I told her."

Jade's eyes became perfectly round. "And how did you know?"

"I read it in the paper."

"You did?" Lemon asked.

"Yes. There was an article just after Mr. Nichols death. It talked about how Lemon Lister had been seen at his home while the police were still there. And the reporter who saw Ms. Lister asked an officer who informed him that Ms. Lister was Mr. Nichols's dog walker, and when the reporter asked after the dog the officer told her that Ms. Lister had taken possession of the dog, just as she had with Ms. Ross's dog."

"Holy shit." Jade slumped back in the chair, her hand slipping away from Lemon this time.

"Ma'am?"

"Thanks for your help. Melanie," Jade said. "That's all we needed."

"Of course. Please let me know if there is anything else I can do for you." Melanie's voice echoed bright and sunny before the line went dead.

"What?" Lemon asked. "What's going on?"

"Don't you see?" Jade threw her arms in the air. "You were publicly identified as having George and Jillian's dogs."

"So what? What does Snickers and Klee have to do with anything?"

"It means you were in the house to get the dog. It means you could have the letter. It means," Jade grasped Lemon's hand again. She squeezed hard enough to cause a flicker of pain as Lemon's bones practically ground together. "You could be targeted by the killer."

CHAPTER TWENTY

Detective Zahn's lips turned down so hard that deep lines formed on either side of his mouth. "Back up, ladies. You've been trying to track down the killer on your own?"

No one was going to fire Lemon from being a dog walker for sticking her nose where it didn't belong. But Jade was at risk here, and Lemon had the deep desire to defend her. Only she had no idea how. Her tongue stuck to the roof of her mouth as if it had been glued there by the savvy detective himself.

"Yes." Jade's spine was ramrod straight.

Beside her, Mei actually grinned. "Yes, sir."

Detective Zahn pointed his exasperated expression at Lemon next. But she was unable to speak. She couldn't lie to anyone well, especially not a cop.

"Why would you do that?" His question hit like a prizefighter landing his punch.

"We just wanted to help." Lemon's words squeezed through her voice box in a high-pitched whisper.

Detective Zahn expelled a massive sigh. "Okay, well, let me tell you what I know."

Mei shifted from arms folded to hands on her knees, leaned forward, instantly on alert. "Please do."

Detective Zahn—in what might have been a first in his entire career—chuckled. "A little eager, are we?"

Lemon glanced over at Jade. Her expression reflected what Lemon could only describe as contrite. "We just want to make sure no one else dies."

"Well, as I'm sure you've already deduced, that's what I want, too."

A sense of hope rose in Lemon's heart. Despite her perception of reality attempting to seep into this situation, she couldn't help but play out her fantasy that Detective Zahn would offer to share every detail the police had gathered, at which point she, Mei, and Jade—okay, mostly Mei and Jade—would provide the key clue that would solve the entire case.

From the moment she'd met him, Detective Zahn presented as someone's slightly cranky, but very loving, grandpa. The impression affected every interaction Lemon had with him. And despite the seriousness of this conversation, that image of him continued to plague her.

"You first," he said.

Jade sighed, but obliged the detective. "Here's the thing. We're pretty sure Jillian and George's killer is after a letter that has gone missing. And we think the media has managed to imply that Lemon may be one of the people in possession of this letter. So we're assuming the killer knows about the letter and wants to get a hold of it. And if that's the case, and that's why they broke into Ms. McBride's office, then perhaps Lemon is in danger."

Lemon's knee bounced up and down as she awaited Detective Zahn's reaction to Jade's explanation for why they had asked to meet with him. Her eyes roamed his face, from the prickly salt and pepper stubble on his chin to the dark shadows underlining his wise, brown eyes.

Detective Zahn smiled just the tiniest bit, enough to convey a gentleness. "I'm aware of the break-in as well as the possibility there may be some sort of documentation involving Jillian Ross the perpetrator was searching for. Do you, Ms. Lister," he turned to the side to focus on

Lemon, "know what the contents of this letter are?"

"No, I have no idea." Lemon swallowed hard. "It was Helen McBride who told me about it. She said it was a thing for rich people to give their lawyer secret letters. I honestly don't have a clue."

A hard puff of air exploded through Zahn's lips as his eyes turned up toward the ceiling. "That's unfortunate."

Jade tapped the table with her finger. "No one has even so much as an inkling what's in this letter? But for some reason, McBride thinks it's important enough for someone to break into her office to get it? There must be some theory as to what it contains."

Zahn leaned the chair back. The tuna can-sized room in the crime lab provided no space, and his chair slammed against the wall. Instead of startling and dropping back to all four feet, he ignored the jarring movement and remained relaxed, resting his head against the plaster behind him. "No real theories at the moment. Do you have any?"

"Cops." Jade said. "Always answering a question with a question."

Zahn chuckled. "Okay, Crime Lab. 'Cause you never do that."

"But," Lemon's voice was far less confident and jovial than her companions, "does no one really know why this letter is so important?"

Zahn set his chair back on the floor. "Only that Jillian gave a sealed envelope to her attorney three days prior to her death, saying she was to hold onto it until Jillian instructed her to hand deliver it to George Nichols. When Jillian died, Helen McBride delivered the letter to Mr. Nichols without ever opening it. Then Mr. Nichols was killed and the letter cannot be located. The assumption is that whatever is in that envelope was of great importance to both Ms. Ross and Mr. Nichols and therefore may also have been important to the killer—assuming they were both killed by the same person."

"Don't you think they were?" Jade asked.

"We don't have any evidence to corroborate that at this time." Zahn rubbed his chin, the sound like sandpaper against linen. "We also don't have any evidence that rules it out."

Lemon twisted her fingers together in her lap. "What should we do now?"

"You," Zahn pointed his finger at Jade, "need to keep your eyes on your work in the lab. And you." He pointed his finger at Lemon. "Stay quiet and careful. I don't want you caught up in looking for a person this dangerous."

The sensation of being reprimanded by a sweet great uncle with her best intentions in mind overwhelmed Lemon. She turned from Zahn to meet Jade's gaze. She was sure she would see the same fiery determination Jade had displayed from day one. But when her gaze finally locked with Jade's, shock ran through Lemon. No fierce commitment to the truth at all costs greeted her. Instead, fear and concern dominated the soft expression on her face. She frowned. "Yes, detective, you're right. We need to keep Lemon safe."

This answer seemed to satisfy Zahn. He didn't bother to check in with Lemon to see if she, too agreed to the rules. That Lemon was not the one to lead the charge into battle must have been apparent to him from the beginning. If Jade agreed, Zahn thought he could rest easy. Lemon wouldn't kick up a fuss.

Lemon managed to work up the strength to form a half-smile. "Thank you for meeting with us, Detective Zahn."

He nodded brusquely before wrenching himself out of the chair. Watching his shuffling sidestep as he worked his way out of the cramped room might have been amusing if so much wasn't at stake.

The moment the door closed behind Zahn, Jade jumped up, abandoning her little plastic chair so dispassionately she didn't even flinch when it hit the wall behind her. Lemon cringed, but there was little time for any other reaction because Jade hauled her up by the elbow and pulled her into a massive bear hug.

The official plastic badge Jade wore clashed with the smaller "visitor" badge stuck to Lemon's chest. The two pieces clicked together as Jade shifted to squeeze Lemon, then pressed their lips together. The kiss was not sweet, as it had been before. Nor was it passionate. Desperation rode the wave between their bodies and their mouths.

The adrenaline-driven response did strange things to Lemon's brain. Thoughts rolled in at hyper-speed. But instead of being blurred, each one flashed crystal clear, like a high-definition picture. Fear stood there between them. It was in the kiss Jade gave her, the idea of things left unsaid and undone. The sheer terror of a life stopped short, as Jillian's had been. As George's had been.

That thought sped away, making room for the next. Fear nowhere near as intense as that coursing through her veins now had prevented Lemon from doing so many things in life, including enjoying this long-awaited second kiss with Jade. It had prevented her from making her own choices, from following her heart.

But everything was different now. No matter the consequences, Lemon would step up. For the first time in her life, she would do exactly what she wanted to do, what she needed to do. She would prove to herself—perhaps even at the cost of proving it to other people—that she could solve this puzzle.

****

Lemon's dry lip chafed against the compostable lid of the cup holding her latte. The liquid concentrated through the small hole burned her lip. She pulled the cup away from her and peeled off the lid. As she blew across the creamy tan liquid, Lemon's eyes peered over the rim at her partner in crime.

"I know this is important, but I'm not super into getting caught with this." Mike pressed his thumb against the sensor on his tablet before sliding it across the table to Lemon. "It's all on here. I have no idea if IT will figure out I downloaded it."

"You're doing the right thing." Lemon spared him a glance before turning her attention to the screen.

Mike's voice, low and husky, dropped to a half-whisper. "This was everything I found that mentioned both my mother and George Nichols in the company files."

Lemon slid her finger down the side bar and slowly scrolled through a series of emails, her eyes scanning one side to the other as she searched for highlighted names and made notes of dates.

"It doesn't amount to much, I'm afraid," Mike said. "About twenty emails my mother sent from the company server to George and a handful that mention George when talking to other people."

They'd started with the oldest email, dating back a few years. Benign communications mentioning little things about the museum or asking for the name or number of a mutual acquaintance.

Mike's fingers drummed impatiently on the table as he waited for Lemon to finish. "I didn't find anything significant in the direct messages between them. But, if you go to the end, there's a message dated two days before mom died."

Lemon lifted her head. "How's that possible? I thought she retired almost two years ago."

"She did. But people inside the company still wrote to her. In the case of the last few messages on there." Mike pointed at the tablet. "Since they originated in a company email, they are on the server, even though the messages were sent to mom's personal address."

Lemon followed Mike's instructions and scrolled until she reached the email sent to Jillian two days before her death. Lemon's eyes flew over the words hungrily hoping to find some little gem of information. The email was short and cryptic.

> *Dear J-*
> *You need to settle things with George Nichols. He's*
> *going to win this battle. Your moves against him are*
> *causing a lot of attention. No one's asking you to*
> *contribute to the purchase. Just let it happen. Stand*
> *down. Please.*
> *-Tom*

"Who's Tom?"

"The company lawyer," Mike said.

Lemon schooled her features, hoping to contain her own thoughts as she played ignorant with her next question. "And the 'purchase?' What's that?"

"My guess," Mike waved at the tablet with his coffee cup, "it's the painting mom and George were fighting over. The one the museum bought."

No point in pretending now that Mike confirmed her suspicions, Lemon's flat tone sounded disturbing even to her own ears. "The one that's being dedicated to George Nichols at the exhibit opening on Saturday?"

"Yeah. The way I read this." Mike took the tablet back. "Tom didn't want the company caught in the crossfire of mom's battle with George over the painting."

"But wasn't it kind of all over by then?" Lemon asked. "I mean, by the time this email was written, George had already raised the money to purchase the painting for the museum. Like a week after this was written the thing was hung in the museum. I thought the battle was basically finished then, and your mom lost."

"She did. I mean, the board voted against her and the purchase was already a done deal, pretty much. All that was left was payment. Which happened just days after she died. So yeah, it was over."

"Then why was Tom asking her to cool it?"

Mike folded his hands together over the tablet, as if protecting its contents. "I can't ask Tom, for obvious reasons."

"Like, he'd know you got the emails from the server?"

"Yeah. And I need my job. Family company or not. I can still get canned."

Lemon frowned. She hadn't intended to put Mike's job at risk when she asked him to see if he could find anything out at the company. "Sorry."

"Don't be. The point is, since I couldn't ask him directly, I went to another source."

"Oh yeah, who?"

A sly smile crept across his lips. "Tom's executive assistant is kind of one of my exes. It didn't end badly. Emma and I stayed friends. Don't tell my wife, though. She's kind of a nightmare about my exes."

Lemon repressed the urge to tell Mike that didn't surprise her. "So you asked her what she knew about it?"

"Yep. And she actually had the goods."

"She did?"

"Uh huh. Turns out Tom bitched extensively to Emma about my mom and George's feud and how it was affecting the company's image, especially among the rich and gossipy."

Lemon scooted to the edge of her seat. "Yeah? So, what did she say?"

"Apparently, Tom had gotten on mom's case about it earlier on. But when the board voted against mom, he calmed down about it. Then he found out she was making a move to stop the purchase from going through."

"A move. What kind of move?"

"Don't know. No one seems to. Not even Helen."

"You talked to her, too?"

Mike rubbed his cheek with his palm. "I did. She's pretty freaked out about everything right now. Told me to leave it all alone. Let the police figure it out."

"I've been hearing that a lot lately, too."

"Well, you know what I say?"

Lemon stared straight into Mike's eyes. They gleamed with a mischievous spark. "What?"

"Screw it. We're solving this."

CHAPTER TWENTY-ONE

The yelping sound echoing through the dog park struck Lemon in the gut. No one responsible for a dog ever wanted to hear that guttural sound of pain. But as she turned her attention toward the sound, the feeling of guilt morphed into something else.

The dog that made the unmistakable shriek was one of her own. Klee—a soft whine having replaced the ear-splitting cry—ambled toward her, his front paw held up as he hopped along on his remaining three feet.

"There's a hole here. Oh my God, he fell into it. I saw him just tumble." A man in shorts and a sweatshirt ran toward the place Klee had fallen. From a different direction a woman rushed out to meet him there, both peering at the hole.

While the observers to the tragedy fell to their knees to examine the pit, Lemon scooped Klee up in her arms. After a quick kiss to his snout, she gingerly placed her finger and thumb on his paw, but he yelped, wiggling against her. She abandoned the idea of touching the paw. Seeing no visible blood, she clutched him to her chest, holding the rest of him steady.

The two onlookers helped her gather up the rest of the dogs and get them settled in the back of the van. Once she was alone in the front with Klee curled up on the passenger seat beside her, the panic really took over. She frantically rifled through the packed glove compartment, dislodging a few oil change receipts before extracting a manila folder.

Lemon sighed in relief. "See Klee, your new mommy managed to do something right. Because I forgot to take your vet info out of here, we don't have to go back to the house. We're going straight to the vet." She put the van in gear and did her best not to speed too much as she headed to the clinic.

Half-hour later, she handed Klee to a vet tech in purple scrubs and turned to Ken, the receptionist at the front desk. He pressed a hand over hers. "It'll be okay. We'll take good care of Klee. I'll take you back in to see him as soon as we get the x-rays. Do you have other dogs in the van?" He pointed out the window to the van with the giant "Doggo Dilly's" painted on the side. "Do you need to get them out of there?"

"I do, and if we're here too long, I will. The air is on now and they should be good for a little while longer."

"Okay. Well, let me know." He turned back to the computer. "You know, I think Klee still has insurance and he's fully covered."

"He does, thank God," Lemon said. With trembling hands, she threw open the cover to the folder and stared down at the short stack of paper.

Lemon flipped over each sheet as she identified it. She found the insurance paperwork and handed it to Ken. She might have closed the folder again, ignoring the small item tucked just behind her target. Instead, she stared down at it, her heart hammering.

"Okay, Lemon, take a seat. I'll let you know as soon as Klee is out of x-ray."

Clutching the folder in her hands, Lemon managed to back into a chair, flopping down and returning her attention to the packet.

No longer sealed, the ragged edge invited Lemon to check out its contents. She examined the front of the envelope. There was no mistake. Blue ink pen identified the intended recipient as George Nichols.

The bell above the door dinged with the sound of another pet parent arriving, but it only barely registered above the whoosh of heavy breathing echoing in her ears. The paper crinkled as she slid it open. Her heart beat in distinct thumps as she read every word, then read it again.

By the time Ken called her, Lemon had slipped the letter back into its envelope and secured it back in the folder. She gripped the folder as if it were a greased pig attempting to slip out of her grasp as she rose and followed the vet tech.

Everything. Absolutely everything had just changed.

The E-collar struck Lemon's thigh. She grasped the edge of the plastic cone surrounding Klee's head and gently settled it back on her lap. Reaching inside the clear plastic, she stroked his head. Still half-drugged, his eyes lulled sleepily. "Stay still, baby. Just for a little while longer."

The leather beneath her squeaked as she shifted under Klee's weight. With Jade's help, all the other dogs made it safely to their homes, but she couldn't bear to leave Klee with only Snickers as his nurse. In addition to sporting the cone of shame, he wore a fresh new cast on his front right foot. And he was high as a kite.

So with Jade having handled the crew of client dogs, and now heading to Lemon's house to take care of Snickers, Lemon had hopped into a cab that took her to a glass-covered high-rise in the Financial District.

The fifteenth-floor lobby was austere. The receptionist wore the deepest frown Lemon had ever seen. "You can't bring that dog in here, ma'am."

Lemon glanced around the brown and cream-colored, leather-soaked room. The only audience was an older woman wearing a flowery dress, sitting patiently on a couch behind her. The woman smiled sweetly at Lemon and Klee.

"He just left the ER, poor thing. I can't leave him alone. You must understand. I'm sure you have a dog, right?"

The man glanced at the waiting woman before glaring back at Lemon and releasing a heavy sigh. "I guess. Please take a seat over there."

Sitting on the stiff chair in the corner, Lemon ran through every piece of information she'd stumbled upon in the last few weeks. George and Jillian's long connection. Their former friendship. Jillian's trust of George, as evidenced by her leaving money with him. Their recent feud over a one-of-a-kind painting. The letter Jillian left for George. All of it had come together in this moment.

For what must have been the twentieth time since she settled into this leather cocoon in the marble and steel lobby of Lucas Johns Art Specialists, she ran her hand over the exterior of her jacket. Through the wind-resistant fabric, her fingers identified the crinkle of paper. Still there.

"Ms. Lister."

Lemon's head snapped up to see the receptionist, his neck craned to peer at her over his high desk while he remaining seated. She stood carefully, taking care to ensure Klee didn't get too jostled.

Only when she reached the counter did the man stand. He shot a glare at Klee before walking around the desk toward a wide hallway. Without sparing a glance over his shoulder, he marched past a row of doors, each with a shiny brass plate identifying the person inside.

Too busy working to match his fast pace while keeping Klee as steady as possible, Lemon didn't get the chance to read any of the names identified on the doors. But none of them were their destination because the man didn't stop until he reached the end of the hall, where a single door blocked entrance to what was presumably an office, much like the green curtain obscuring the inner workings at Oz. The brass plate on the door was no bigger or more ornamental than the others, but somehow it shined a little brighter, cast a bigger imprint on the faces looking at it from the confines of the hallway – Lucas Johns.

The receptionist knocked lightly and received an immediate reply. He opened the door and stepped aside, gesturing with one arm as if he were a game show host. Lemon slipped past him, shielding Klee from his harsh gaze.

She registered the change in atmosphere as her feet fell on the soft cushion of carpeting vastly different from the hard, slick marble of the hall. Natural light from massive floor-to-ceiling windows created a bright showroom for the remaining walls, which were coated in artwork.

A tall, lean man with a head of thick, black hair stood as Lemon shuffled toward a wooden desk the size of a small yacht perched like an alter in the center of the room. He skirted the furniture gracefully to meet her with an outstretched arm. "Ms. Lister, I'm Lucas Johns."

Lemon extracted one hand from Klee, securing him in the cradle of her other arm, and shook Lucas John's hand. "Call me Lemon."

His smile oozed charm. "And call me, Lucas. Please sit down." He pointed to a wingback chair.

Lemon lowered herself into the chair and settled Klee on her lap. After a little fussing he managed to find a way to get comfortable with the stupid cone cradling his head and heavy cast on his leg. He closed his eyes with a snorty sigh.

"Sorry about the dog. He had an accident this morning, and I couldn't leave him."

With far warmer eyes than the receptionist, Lucas peered at Klee before taking a seat across from her. "No problem. I happen to love dogs. Though I don't have one of my own. I hope he's all right."

"He will be. He actually belonged to George Nichols. See, I am— was both George and Jillian Ross's dog walker. And now, well, I have both of their dogs, and that's basically how I got here. To you."

A shadow crossed Lucas's face. He leaned back in his chair, tenting his fingers in front of him. "I see."

"So, it appears that Jillian left a letter with her lawyer for George. And when she died, the lawyer gave it to George. And then when George died the letter went missing." Lemon paused, examining Lucas's face. Whatever he was thinking remained a mystery. Blank and untelling, Lucas John's face was made for a Vegas poker table.

"Interesting. So this letter is missing?"

"Well, not anymore. I happened to find it about an hour ago when I was at the vet with Klee."

All passivity fled Lucas's face so quickly it threw Lemon off-kilter.

"Really?" He sat up straight in his chair, hands landing on the polished desk.

"Yeah. And I read it. And it mentions you. And that's why I'm here."

Lucas dropped his head into his hands. Long fingers rubbed circles at his temples, knuckles brushing against curly black hair, making it puff out from the sides like jellyfish swimming frantically for the surface.

When he raised his head again, eyes weary, he sighed so hard it sounded like a windstorm in the big room. "I'm guessing it was about my opinion on the ancient Roman easel painting."

Lemon pulled the envelope out of its hiding spot and handed it to Lucas. "Honestly, I didn't fully understand it. It was like it started in the middle of a conversation. But if I had to guess, yeah, that's what I think it's about. That's why I'm here."

Lucas slid his finger between the ragged edges of the envelope, then pushed the two sides open using his thumb. Slowly, as if he were walking to his doom, he pulled the letter out and opened it. He meticulously straightened the folded paper on the surface of his desk before finally scanning it.

Lemon tracked each breath that filled her lungs. Her hands remained still, intertwined in Klee's soft fur. Her gaze stayed pinned to Lucas Johns' face.

When he finally reached the end of the letter, Lucas took another few excruciating moments to sit with his eyes closed before meeting Lemon's gaze. "Well, I was afraid of this."

"Afraid of what?"

"That all of this really was about the painting." Lucas released the letter, allowing it to settle on his desk. "As you read, I told Jillian I thought the painting was a fake. But I refused to make my opinion public."

Lemon hunched forward slightly, but realized her mistake when Klee's cone cut into her thigh. She slumped back in the chair. "Why? Why would you keep it a secret? Especially with the museum about to spend millions on it?"

Lucas's gazed at the desk before fixating on a location somewhere over Lemon's shoulder. "Because everyone on that board uses my agency to appraise art, and so do all the donors George Nichols got to give money toward the purchase. By the time Jillian contacted me with her suspicions and I confirmed them for myself…well, it was too damn late. I didn't want to get involved."

"But you told Jillian what you really thought?"

"I told her. And I told her I wouldn't put it in writing. I told her the ship had sailed, and she needed to let it go."

"But she wouldn't, would she?" Lemon said.

"No, and to be honest, I would have eventually stood behind her. But she died."

"She was killed. And I'm pretty sure it was over this painting."

Lucas pressed his eyes closed and swiped at them with his hand. "This." He slammed his hand onto the paper in front of him. "Pretty much proves that. She left this letter for George, telling him what I really thought of the painting. She was killed and so was he."

Lemon let out a deep breath. Her shoulders suddenly felt lighter and far more tense. "So, if that's what we both believe, what are we going to do about it?"

Lucas met her withering stare. "Have you contacted the police about this letter yet?"

"No. I came here first. I wanted to know what I had."

"The smoking gun, I'd say. But I wonder what Detective Zahn will say."

Lemon's eyes nearly popped out of her head. "You know Detective Zahn?"

"He's talked to literally everyone about this case. Me included."

"But you didn't tell him about the painting?"

"I did. But I wasn't clear."

"What does that mean?"

"I told him what he already knew. That Jillian and George were fighting over the painting. He never asked if either them wanted me to appraise it. And I didn't offer up the information. I'm not proud of what I did." Lucas's gaze fell to the sleeping dog in Lemon's arms. Something crossed his features. Whether it was Klee's generally pathetic appearance with his purple cast and satellite cone or just guilt over leaving the pup an orphan, she couldn't completely discern. "But I'm ready now. No matter what the consequences are."

"Okay." Lemon felt as though they stood on a precipice, looking down at a deadly fall or across it at safety and freedom. She clutched Klee as Lucas pulled out a business card and, glancing between it and the phone, dialed a number.

The phone had a speaker feature that allowed the dull ring to echo through the office. "SFPD, how can I help you?"

"I'm trying to reach Detective Zahn. I thought I was calling his direct line."

"Oh, you were," the woman's voice said. "But he has it forwarded. He's not in right now. Can I take a message?"

Lucas's eyes shifted from the phone to Lemon. She gave him a pert nod, not knowing exactly what she was supposed to be conveying in that gesture. But he seemed to find direction there.

With a commanding tone he said, "This is Lucas Johns. I have information regarding the double murder he is investigating, and I need to speak with him at his earliest convenience."

"Hold please." Those two words were all they got before the line clicked and soft music took the place of the woman's voice.

For some reason, both Lemon and Lucas ended up staring at Klee during that musical interlude. Unfazed by the attention, Klee continued his slumber, his chest rising and falling in Lemon's arms, his warm breath hitting her wrist in a regular pattern.

"What happened to his leg?" Lucas asked.

"We were at the dog park and he was running full tilt, chasing his terrier bestie when he fell into a hole some other dog must have dug. He was moving so fast the momentum kind of carried his body forward while his foot stayed stuck in the hole. Poor baby."

"Ouch. Is he going to be okay?"

"Yeah. It was a clean break. The vet says he should heal up just fine."

Lucas nodded and redirected his gaze at the phone, while Lemon gently stroked Klee's spine.

"Mr. Johns?" The woman's voice, far more strained now, came back suddenly.

"Yes. I'm here."

"I have Detective Zahn on the line for you. I'm going to transfer you. If you get disconnected, please call me right back, and I will get you re-connected, okay?"

"Okay."

Another pause, this one short and silent. Then Detective Zahn answered. "Zahn here."

"Detective Zahn, it's Lucas Johns. I'm in my office and I have Lemon Lister with me."

"Oh, really? And why's that?" Zahn asked.

"She found the letter."

The silence on the other line nearly exploded Lemon's brain. It seemed to last an eternity.

Finally, Zahn spoke. "I see. I'm sending a cruiser. Just sit tight."

CHAPTER TWENTY-TWO

Lemon's hand shook so hard the phone wobbled, making it difficult to type out a text. But she pressed on, her thumb roaming over the letters one at time.

"Say that you're on your way and it's essential she keep everyone who works in her department there." Detective Zahn tried to get a better view of her phone screen.

In the back of the police cruiser beside the detective, with a Basset Hound at her feet and the over six-foot Lucas Johns in the seat in front of her, Lemon developed a case of sudden onset claustrophobia.

"Okay. But she's going to ask to why," Lemon said.

"One thing at a time," Zahn said.

"He's very good at this." The officer driving the car had been praising every sentence out of Detective Zahn's mouth since they left the station and began this crazy journey of errands.

This last leg of their trip had amped up her anxiety about a thousand-fold, especially now that she was being instructed to send cryptic messages to Mei.

The first ride, to drop Klee off at the vet's for safe keeping until after this nightmare ended, wasn't too bad. The second trip, to retrieve Milo from Ron's house was a little weirder. And now they were on route to the Legion of Honor and she was supposed to get her best friend—who was definitely the low person on the totem pole—to convince everyone in the antiquities department to stay put until they arrived.

The good news was that the museum was closing soon, meaning they had at least fifteen minutes before anyone working even thought about leaving, since they had to get all the guests out first. The even better news was that the grand opening of the new antiquities exhibit was happening tomorrow so no one in the antiquities department would be leaving early tonight.

Nevertheless, it was a weird text to send, and as she expected, Mei responded with a slew of question marks. Lemon tilted her screen to show Zahn.

"Write that you are on your way."

"That's it?" Lemon asked. "Just that I'm on my way?"

"Trust him," the officer driving said.

Zahn might be a great detective, but that didn't make him some sort of texting genius, especially not when it came to communications between two twenty-something bffs. But she did as he asked.

As soon as Lemon hit send as the car took a sharp turn into the parking lot for the museum. It became immediately clear to Lemon that her texts were completely pointless. She glared at Zahn.

He simply shrugged and stared out the window at the half-dozen police cars positioned around the museum. As they parked, Lemon spotted several uniformed officers clearing the place of visitors as if they were conducting a fire drill.

The people pouring out of the museum had terror painted on their faces. They hurried away from the building as if it might blow at any moment.

"Why did I need to text Mei if you sent the cavalry?" Lemon asked.

"Because all this," Zahn waved his hand toward the building. "Is not being advertised inside. For most of the employees, it's just a regular closing time. Ready?" He put his hand on the door handle and looked pointedly at the dog draped over Lemon's feet.

"You don't feel the least bit guilty about employing Ron's dog to help us without asking? I mean, Ron's in there right now. In the antiquities department. And we just stole his dog.”

“Nope. Ready?”

Lemon sighed. The sweet middle-aged detective had turned into Dirty Harry at some point on their trip across the city. He even wore his gun on his hip now instead of tucked into a holster on his shoulder. The new look took him from Columbo to Stabler in an instant. “Come on, Milo. Time to put that nose of yours to work.”

She stepped out of the car, dragging a reluctant hound with her. The officer who’d been driving stared down at the Basset. “Sir, are you sure you don’t want me to call a K-9 unit, one trained to—”

“No,” Zahn said. “Absolutely not. This dog is the one we need.” Zahn then slapped one hand on Lucas Johns’s back. “Ready?”

Lucas nodded and assessed Lemon. She’d managed to get Milo to cooperate, and he now stood beside her waiting for instruction. “We’re ready, I guess.”

Detective Zahn rubbed his hands together. “Let’s do this.”

As they moved toward the Thinker statue in the center of the plaza, a police officer approached Zahn. “Only staff left in the building, sir,” she said.

“Great.” Zahn marched toward the front doors with his makeshift entourage of an art appraiser, a dog walker, and a hound in his wake.

Almost as soon as Lemon was through the front doors, Mei ran toward her. Her approach was so fast Milo let out one loud bark. “What the hell is going on?”

“Damnit.” Zahn said. “I don’t want…certain people to know the dog is here.” Even over Mei’s giant hug Lemon could see the detective frantically looking around.

“Seriously.” Mei took a step away from Milo. “What’s going on?”

“Is everyone in your department still here?” Zahn asked Mei, ignoring the museum director, who was desperately trying to get his attention.

“Yes. All hands on deck for the opening tomorrow,” Mei said.

“Detective,” the museum director spoke loudly in her attempt to gain Zahn's attention.

With no choice but to speak with her, Zahn turned his attention to the director, giving Lemon and Mei a brief moment.

Mei practically vibrated. "Lemon, what the hell is going on?"

"I found the letter, Mei. And it led to him." Lemon pointed to Lucas Johns. He waved from his position a short distance away. "He's Lucas Johns."

"Yeah. I know. You don't go to school for art history and not know who Lucas Johns is." Mei's face went slack, the most ridiculous star-struck expression on her face. It was nearly as bad as the time they ran into a B-actor at a coffee shop on Market street.

"Lister." Suddenly a drill sergeant on top of everything else, Zahn beckoned to Lemon. "Ready?"

"Uh, yeah, sure." Lemon moved to follow Zahn, Milo trotting obediently beside her, Mei shadowing them all.

They passed through the museum's opulent lobby, skipped the rooms filled with Rodin sculptures and headed to the back where the period paintings began. There the museum went in two directions. Zahn took a sharp left, heading through the history section. The artwork got older and older. Still a few rooms away from the new exhibit, the museum director stopped, pivoted and used a keycard to open a door for Zahn.

"We're going into the back?" Mei asked.

Lemon shrugged. "Apparently."

Once they were in the catacombs of the museum's archives, Zahn stopped. He turned on his heel and stared down at Milo, who panted, tongue dripping drool onto the hardwood floor. "How do you make him sniff?"

"I don't know," Lemon said. "He just does it on his own."

"Sir," that same officer—the one that had driven them here—spoke again. "The trained dogs are just a phone call away."

Zahn ignored him and kept his gaze on Milo. "Maybe walk him around or something?"

Lemon wandered through the elaborate shelving system, weaving around wooden structures and steel reinforcements, all holding carefully packed and labeled items. After a few minutes Milo started to sniff, though his enthusiasm was lacking. It almost seemed as if he was doing it out of boredom more than anything else.

Lemon looped around the last set of shelves, finding a row of large crates against the back wall. That's when Milo got down to business, and for a fleeting moment, Lemon imagined that he was about to lift his leg and pee on some priceless work of art.

But then she recognized the signs, or rather felt them, as he tugged on the leash, his broad, muscular body leading the way. This was how it had been in the grove outside the museum when Milo was on a scent.

Lemon's heart raced as she worked to stay with him, tracking every twitch of his powerful nose as it roamed over the nooks and crannies of the crates and the tiny spaces in between.

At the end of the line, where the wall made a ninety-degree turn, Milo stopped. He lifted his front foot and pawed at a large crate. "I think he's found something." Lemon's voice cracked.

The voices that returned were surprisingly close, causing her to jump. She spun to see that everyone—Zahn, Lucas, Mei, the museum director, and the other police officer—all stood behind her in a tight clump, wedged in between all the items, heads poking over shoulders to get a look.

Milo whined and pawed again, breaking off a few slivers of wood. Zahn stepped forward then, sending Lemon and Milo back along the other wall. "Let's open it."

"What's happening?" The voice, deep and loud, nearly shook Lemon's entire being.

Lemon spun to see Ron Killian standing directly behind her. He glanced at his own dog beside her, pressed his lips into a hard line, and glared at Lemon. Completely unable to respond, Lemon stood, breathing fast.

"I have permission to check this building and everything in it," Zahn said. "And I want to see inside that box."

Ron ripped his gaze away from Lemon and pinned it on Zahn. "Fine. Open it then."

Mei and the officer made quick work of pulling the top off the crate and setting it aside.

Everyone in the room—man, woman, and dog—peered inside the dark enclosure only to see absolutely nothing.

"Well, now that we've done that, does anyone want to tell me what you are looking for? Perhaps I can help find it." Ron's tone projected amusement and arrogance mixed with anger in what Lemon thought was a heady and dangerous cocktail.

Despite Ron's authoritative presence, Zahn completely ignored him. "Ms. Lister. Please continue."

Unsure how to fulfill the detective's unrealistic expectations, Lemon tried her best to play act a sniffer dog handler, a real challenge since she was neither a handler nor was Milo a trained scent detection dog. "Um, sniff Milo."

Ron chuckled. "Did it occur to you that *my* dog may just be sniffing out things that *I've* touched.

"Get that crate tested for blood," Zahn said to the police officer behind him. The man practically ran out of the room.

Despite Ron's assertion that his dog was tracking his scent, Milo was wholly uninterested in him. He stuck his nose to the ground and pulled Lemon behind him as if he were a motor boat and she were his water skier.

The crowd followed behind Lemon, giving her the distinct impression that she was a celebrity with her own entourage. With her one and only chance to experience that level of attention trained on her Lemon became filled with anxiety. She sent a secret message to Milo that she hoped would travel down his leash, past his floppy ears, and into his brain. *Please do something magical, you amazing creature.*

Uninterested in anything happening around him, Milo stayed focused on the scents penetrating his powerful nose. He followed whatever it was that struck his olfactory organ with an unrelenting determination. He dragged Lemon and the rest of his fans through the back room, darting and weaving through boxes and crates.

Despite his short legs and his breed's reputation for being lazy, Milo used every fiber of his being to keep his body following his nose. Lemon fought to keep up with him, suffering a few scrapes to her legs along the way.

Milo took an abrupt turn, pressing his nose against the door and whining. Lemon quickly pushed the door open, allowing him to shuffle through it, stick his nose back to the floor and follow his invisible trail into the public part of the museum.

Milo took his congregation on a tour of the older artworks. He sped them through the first five centuries of the modern era in reverse. He plunged into the ancient world exhibit, straining against his harness, nearly knocking Lemon off her feet.

The hound practically inhaled the coating on the hardwood floors as he moved past marble statues and ornate frescoes. He didn't pause at the new centerpiece of the exhibit. Milo passed underneath the priceless ancient painting as if it were a boring old tree on the way to a highly valued fire hydrant.

It wasn't until Milo reached the very back of the room, the end of the museum wing itself that he seemed to find his prize. He reached the sarcophagus, running his nose around the entire base, then raising his head up to sniff along the stone side.

And that's when it happened. Milo let out a low howl, reached out one paw and scraped it frantically against the stone.

Lemon spun around, coming nose-to-nose with detective Zahn. He shouldered past her, stepping up to the sarcophagus. "Open it."

"Really, detective," Ron said. "When you opened the last empty crate that was one thing. But now you want to ruin an ancient artifact in this useless experiment?"

"I give permission for you to open it," the museum director said, her voice loud and firm.

"Let's do it." Zahn stepped back and pulled Lemon with him.

Lemon squatted on the floor, yanking Milo away from the sarcophagus and holding his broad body against her chest.

The museum personnel present had multiplied significantly. Now at least half a dozen of them, Mei included, worked to remove the lid of the sarcophagus. They worked carefully, taking their time to find the seal and lift the lid with care.

The audience buzzed with impatience Lemon didn't share. She stroked Milo's broad back and tickled his chest. Nothing good came from his last discovery and Lemon had a feeling this time would be the same. She wasn't anxious to see the result.

None of this was Milo's fault, despite the ice-cold glare he received from his owner. Milo was a dog, doing what he was bred to do. Lemon kissed his head, he turned and gave her a sloppy slurp in return.

Eventually, the lid came off. Even as the staff carefully placed it on a tarp on the floor, the detective, the museum director, and a few of the police officers present pressed in, peering into the cavern. And as a sharp scent wafted out of the container and hit each one, their faces contorted.

"What's that?" Zahn asked.

The museum director spoke, her voice shaky. "It appears to be a bed sheet."

Zahn slipped a glove onto one hand, the snap of the latex against his wrist echoing through the cold, marble and stone space. He reached in and pulled gently on something Lemon couldn't see.

Lemon didn't need to look at what lie in that sarcophagus. The collective gasp that exploded in the room told her what she needed to know. The hands clasped over mouths, people pressed in, then quickly moving away. The putrid smell that burned her nose. It was obvious that a footless Jillian Ross had been just been found.

Zahn said, "Ron Killian, you are under arrest for the murder of Jillian Ross." He waved his hand and a police officer droned Miranda rights and slapped cuffs on Ron while everyone else attempted to collect themselves. When the officer finished, Zahn stared straight at Ron. "You have anything to say before we take you away?"

Instead of meeting his gaze, Ron turned his cold glare to Lemon. "You can keep that dog."

CHAPTER TWENTY-THREE

"Okay, start from the beginning." Mei cradled the wine glass in her hands and leaned across the kitchen island toward Jade. Lemon bumped her hip to get her to move a few inches so she could open the utensil drawer and pull out three spoons.

Jade said, "Okay, so Jillian went to the museum to confront Ron. They arranged a meeting early in the morning. No one else was there."

Lemon dropped the spoons on the island between Mei and Jade and went to the cupboard to pull out three bowls. "And that's where he killed and dismembered her?"

"He killed her in the museum, strangulation." Jade said. "Then he tried to fit her in the sarcophagus."

"But why?" Lemon lined the bowls up in a row on the counter.

"He didn't have time to get her out of there and he couldn't risk being seen by a camera or a person, Jade said. "He was safe from prying eyes. But only back there. So he put her in the sarcophagus, but it was too short."

Mei said, "Because people were short back then."

"True. Anyway. He used whatever stuff they have, removed the feet, cleaned up, and buried the feet in the woods behind the museum. All before anyone else showed up for the day."

Mei shivered. "Like me. Yikes. I can't believe there was a dead body in my exhibit the whole damn time."

Lemon pulled a carton of her favorite ice cream out of the freezer. Three dogs lined up at her feet. "So then George finds out her secret."

"Yes," Jade said. "According to Lucas Johns, after piecing it all together, it was Ron himself who faked the painting, the buyer, everything. He planned to keep the money for himself. And when George found out, well, he must have confronted Ron."

"Which would explain why George was such a dick to you that day," Mei told Lemon. "He'd just come from this intense confrontation with Ron."

Lemon tried to keep her emotions in check. She decided the best way was to make the ice cream scoops extra-large.

Jade eyed the ice cream with a smile. "Then Ron killed George. Apparently, he got George into one of the museum vans, killed him and stuffed him in a big packing crate in the back of the van. Just like we thought the killer might have done. And just as we thought, he drove to the marina and used the crate Milo pinged on in the back room to get the body on the boat." Wholly uninterested in fame, Milo kept his attention on the spoon in Lemon's hand moving from the ice cream carton to the bowls.

Mei asked, "But is there any real evidence it was him? I mean besides the coincidences and the motive?"

"Yes." Jade held up one finger. "His blood was found on a nail in the crate that transported George's body. And George's DNA was found in the crate."

"He could have cut his finger another time," Mei said. "Hell, my blood is probably in that back room somewhere."

"Yes, but when you combine that with the crate being missing on that exact day as evidenced by an inventory photo that just happened to be taken and the eye witness account of the man at the marina who saw—and has now identified—Ron moving the crate onto the boat, it makes a better case."

Mei spooned a bite of ice cream. "What about Jillian? I mean, he could argue someone else at the museum did it,"

Jade stuck her own spoon into the ice cream. "But he was the only one there at the time she had to have been put in the sarcophagus—based on when Lemon found the feet. And he has the best motive. The same motive tied to George's murder. And we found his DNA on the sheet she was wrapped up in. He's all done."

Lemon grabbed her own bowl of ice cream before rounding the island and dropping down in the barstool beside Jade. All three dogs lay in a pile at her feet. "Well, I'm glad it's all over."

"And now you have three dogs and a roommate who's afraid of them." Jade laughed.

Mei stuck out her tongue. "I'm getting better. And I'm not afraid of Snickers and Klee anymore, just Milo."

Milo lifted his big head and stared at Mei with his sad, brown eyes. "Seriously, how could anyone be afraid of this sweetheart?" Lemon tickled him under the chin.

Mei scrunched up her nose. "Don't worry about my phobia. I'm dealing with it. The important thing is we're two professional girls living it up in our awesome pad."

Lemon grinned. "I guess I can't complain about being lonely anymore."

Jade leaned over and kissed her sweetly. "I sure hope not."

ACKNOWLEDGEMENTS

This book is my first foray into cozy mystery. It was fun to write, but it was also hard, frustrating, and terrifying. Going from the world of romance to crafting a true whodunnit was a big learning curve. I have to thank Jessie Chandler for editing the manuscript and mentoring me through this process. I also need to thank my publisher, Patty Schramm, for taking a chance on this romance writer with a mystery dream. I wouldn't be where I am in my writing journey without some amazing people who played a role along the way including: Danielle Constein, Rhonna Brown, Kelly Aten, Amy Jambeck, my mom, my auntie, my spouse, and my dog. I love you all!

ABOUT THE AUTHOR

Benna Bos lives in the iconic city of San Francisco with her spouse and her dog. She enjoys placing her characters in this foggy setting and creating stories that weave in the landscape she has come to love. She is obsessed with true crime podcasts, dogs, and museums. Somehow she's lucky enough to get to write about them all.

Bringing rainbow stories to life.

Flashpoint Publications welcomes submissions from writers
of every color and books featuring characters of every color.
In addition, Flashpoint Publications encourages job applicants
of every color whenever a staff position becomes available.
We believe that EVERYONE is entitled to a seat at our table.

www.flashpointpublications.com